Unidentified Flying Oddball

Unidentified Flying Oddball

from the Walt Disney Productions' Film

Book by Vic Crume

Screen Story and Screenplay by Don Tait

Based on Mark Twain's
A Connecticut Yankee in King Arthur's Court

SCHOLASTIC BOOK SERVICES
NEW YORK • TORONTO • LONDON • AUCKLAND • SYDNEY • TOKYO

ISBN 0-590-30061-X

Published by Scholastic Book Services, a division of Scholastic Magazines, Inc., by arrangement with Walt Disney Productions.

12 11 10 9 8 7 6 5 4 3 2 1   9   9/7 0 1 2 3 4/8

To My Readers

1

"Minus five — minus four — three — two — one. Ignition. We have lift-off! Gentlemen — *the bird has flown!*"

In a conference room of Kennedy Space Center, Cape Canaveral, Florida, Dr. Zimmerman held a model spacecraft over his head and added a couple of deep *boom-booms* to give its performance extra realism. Political and military VIPs at Dr. Zimmerman's personally conducted launch almost expected the little model of *Stardust One* to zoom through the conference room ceiling.

The scientist seemed to feel the same way — a little surprised that the toy-sized spaceship was not departing Planet Earth then and there. He began to put *Stardust One* into a slow orbital swing around the only globe handy—his head.

Senator Milburn's first question brought him back to reality. "What'll she do?" he asked bluntly.

The scientist hastily set the model on its little launch-pad. "Oh. The mission of the spacecraft is to explore the stars and planets of this galaxy and beyond, Senator."

"I already know *that*. I mean . . . how fast will she go?"

"Oh, *that*!" Dr. Zimmerman gave up his favorite dream of wandering through the starlit heavens, and got his thoughts on fuel performance. "If our calculations are correct it should definitely exceed relativistic speeds."

"Relativistic? Put it in plain American, Doctor."

Dr. Zimmerman frowned. "Of course! You have heard, I suppose, of Einstein's Theory of Relativity?"

"Just plain talk, please," the Senator demanded firmly.

"Yes, indeed. *Stardust One* should travel faster than light. I am sure you know, Senator, that means traveling faster than 186,283.4 miles per second."

"Wow!" For the first time Senator Milburn

sounded really interested. "That's *really* pouring the coal to it!"

Dr. Zimmerman almost sniffed. "Coal? Our propulsion system is more sophisticated than that, Senator, and quite revolutionary in concept." He crossed over to a wall and raised a blind that had covered a large drawing of the inside and outside of *Stardust One*.

"*Stardust One*," he went on, "will actually collect atoms of the interstellar mediums while in flight. It will ionize the medium ahead of the craft and guide the ions into the intake area — here." He rapped the drawing with his pointer and was about to mention the use of magnetic fields when the Senator interrupted.

"Where'll it go and how long will it take?" he asked.

"In just four and a half years the craft could reach our nearest star, Alpha Centauri, Senator."

A four-star general spoke up. "Doctor Zimmerman — aren't speeds like that supposed to turn back the clock or something?"

The scientist beamed. "That is a fascinating concept, General. Theoretically, a faster-than-light message could be received *before* it is sent. On *Stardust One*, clocks will move more slowly. The crew's hearts will beat more slowly. Their — "

Senator Milburn leaned forward. "Crew? Did I hear you say 'crew'?"

Dr. Zimmerman moved the pointer. "As you see, the ship is designed for two crewmen. Provisions for — "

"You can stop right there, Doctor." The Senator slapped the conference table. "You intend to put *live* men into that untried contraption and just shoot 'em out of this world into who knows where? Oh, no, you're not!"

A hush fell over the table. Dr. Zimmerman looked a little desperate. "*Stardust One has* to be manned, sir. How else will we learn that humans can even *survive* relativistic speeds? Not to mention the craft itself."

The Senator seemed to blast off from some invisible launch-pad of his own. "Oh, no, you don't!" he exclaimed. "You're not going to make guinea pigs out of fine young American men — not while *I'm* representing the government on this project!"

Dr. Zimmerman went pale. His brain whirred. "Well, we do have some women in the space program. Maybe — "

"Fine young *American* women, may I remind you? No sir! You'd better come up with a better brainstorm!" He pointed to little *Stardust One*. "Or *that* baby's never going to get off this table — let alone a launch-pad!"

Like it or not, the conference was over!

* * *

Tom Trimble, computer engineer, hadn't quite got the hang of the lotus position, so highly thought of in yoga mediation. In fact, he meditated more on how to fold his legs properly than on meditating itself. And barely a moment after he'd finally managed to get his ankles properly wedged over his thighs, the office phone jangled. Luckily, his legs had not yet begun to go numb. He untangled them, hit his head on the edge of a drawing board, and reached for the phone. "Trimble here," he answered in his most businesslike voice.

"Trimble? What took you so long? What are you doing?" Dr. Zimmerman asked.

"Yoga, sir," Tom replied truthfully. "But it's my lunch hour."

"I'm taking you off that project, Trimble — "

"Oh, it isn't really a *project*, sir. I'm just interested in — "

"Not *a* project — *the* project!" the Doctor said loudly. "You're going on to humanoids *immediately*. Trimble, I want a robot that walks, talks, sees, feels, reacts. The works. I want it as much like a human as you can make it. And I want it *yesterday*."

Thump. The line went dead.

"Talk about relativistic speeds!" Tom Trimble said angrily at the telephone. "Zimmerman — you're letting your job get to you!"

It wasn't exactly *yesterday*, but Tom Trimble did the next-to-impossible. He designed and built exactly what Dr. Zimmerman needed — the perfect robot.

"We're naming him 'Hermes,'" Tom told the expert who was about to complete the last step — a face for the *Stardust One* robot pilot.

"Hermes?"

"Yep. In honor of the Greek god of travel — *speedy* travel."

"Great idea, Mr. Trimble. Now if you'll just lean back, I'll get a mask of your face. We'll have it on Hermes in no time."

Even Senator Milburn had to marvel at the results of the Trimble creation. It was an absolute look-alike of its inventor! Along with other VIPs, he closely watched the demonstration of Hermes' talents.

"Gentlemen — a few facts," said the scientist. He pinched Hermes' arm.

"Ouch!" came the instant response.

"Please step up and say hello to Hermes." Dr. Zimmerman beamed.

Senator Milburn was first to greet Hermes.

6

"Hello," he said briefly. "What is nine times nine?" He stared keenly at the Trimble-Hermes face.

"Eighty-one," Hermes replied promptly.

The Senator turned to Tom. "Is that right?"

" — Er. Nines were always hard for me, sir."

Congratulations to Dr. Zimmerman flooded the demonstration room for the next ten minutes. Hermes would be launched — and the sooner the better. Then one by one the gentlemen left the room. Hermes and his inventor, Tom Trimble, were already forgotten. "Never mind," Hermes said. "*I* know Dr. Zimmerman didn't build me."

Tom stared at his creation. "Say, Hermes! You are really one smart robot!"

Hermes blinked shyly — he was rather pleased with himself.

2

Launch day arrived and there hadn't been such excitement at the Cape since the very first manned space flight. Outside the Launch Control building Senator Milburn was being congratulated on all sides for demanding the use of a robot. Dr. Zimmerman, though not yet present, was praised by all for his scientific genius.

But the newscaster informing the nation on the progress of the launch was running out of things to say. Hermes, it was true, was already in *Stardust One*. He had looked fit and trim as he'd passed the TV cameras, wearing a sparkling white suit and a dazzling gold helmet. But the only action the newscaster could now observe was in the sky; a tremendous thundercloud was piling up high to the north.

"One moment," said the newscaster into the mike. "We're informed by Ground Control that all systems are 'go,' but we're on hold, due to a technical problem. We're trying to get Dr. Zimmerman for more on that."

Senator Milburn frowned and said, as he strode inside the Launch Control building, "I'll get to the bottom of this or know the reason why."

He found Dr. Zimmerman gazing fixedly at Hermes' image on the screen of the closed circuit TV.

"Hermes," the scientist asked, "where is your sense of patriotism?"

"He wasn't programmed for that, sir," an aide explained.

"Then why wasn't he?" Dr. Zimmerman snapped.

There was no chance to reply, as Senator Milburn came bursting in. "What's holding things up, Zimmerman? I've got important guests out there."

" — Er. We've run into an unexpected problem."

"Now what?"

"Hermes doesn't want to go," the doctor gulped. "He's afraid."

Senator Milburn's jaw nearly hit the carpeting. "Afraid!" he gasped. "How can a pile of nuts and bolts be *afraid*?"

Quickly, Dr. Zimmerman flipped the switch to cut off communication with *Stardust One*. "There is no point in hurting Hermes' feelings," he said coldly.

Little did the Senator worry about feelings — not even Dr. Zimmerman's. "Do you realize the head alone on that thing cost six million dollars? And now you're telling me you've built a prima donna!" He paused. "Can't you disconnect a wire or something?"

"We could, but then we would not have normal human responses. Hermes is programmed to reveal fatigue, tensions, and anxiety. But we didn't expect him to get anxious so soon."

"What's he afraid of?"

"That he won't come back," Dr. Zimmerman answered. "It's a possibility, and Hermes has thought the problem through."

Another aide hurried over. "Walter Cronkite wants to know what's holding things up."

"Tell him it's a technical problem and we're taking care of it."

Senator Milburn stormed to the door. "You'd *better* take care of it. I approved this — this *contraption*. My committee chairmanship is riding on it. You blow it,

10

Zimmerman, and your next year's budget won't be enough to launch a paper airplane!" *Slam!* He went outside.

For a second, Dr. Zimmerman wished he could blast the Senator into the next galaxy. He turned to his aide. "Get Trimble out there to try and talk some sense into Hermes. And snap it up. There's a storm front moving in."

And that was why Tom Trimble, wearing his best blazer, slacks, and moccasins in honor of the special launch day, whisked the three-mile distance from Launch Control over to the restricted area of the launch-pad. At the gantry elevator, Tom, like all well-trained space experts, donned plastic boots as a precaution against carrying Earth dust into *Stardust One*.

"Hermes!" he exclaimed as he entered the main cabin portion of the spaceship. "Why'd you take off your space suit?"

"Don't need it," Hermes replied, staring moodily out a window at the darkening skies.

"I know you don't need it, but Zimmerman thought it was good P.R."

"P.R.?"

"Public Relations."

"Then *you* put it on," Hermes said crossly.

"I don't need it either. But okay. I'll do it just to show you how nice it looks."

While he struggled into the space suit, a heavy roll of thunder reminded him that there was no time to lose. "Hermes," he said sternly, "what's all this nonsense about you not wanting to go?"

"Thirty years is a long time," Hermes replied sulkily.

"Not when you think of it in light years," Tom said cheerfully. "Your batteries are in fine shape, and we've got all kinds of back-up systems. What's there to worry about?"

"That I'm never coming back!" To Tom's horror, Hermes' voice began to quiver.

Tom gulped. "What a silly thing to say! Of *course* you're coming back! Now come on. *You* put on the suit and the helmet, too." But Hermes refused to budge.

Over the launch site ominous stabs of lightning ripped the clouds. "Hermes," Tom begged, "you've put me in a very embarrassing position. Dr. Zimmerman is disappointed in you. Senator Milburn is *very* upset. And *millions* of people are waiting. What are they going to think if we have to scrub this mission because you're afraid — a big robot like you? Now put this on and sit down in your nice chair — it was built just for you." Tom picked up the space suit.

Beneath it was a magazine. A very pretty girl decorated the cover. "Hermes! What are you doing with *this*? Don't you know it might contaminate all outer space?"

Hermes began to pout again. "Well, thirty years *is* thirty years. I only wish I'd picked up a few more!"

"Nonsense." Tom put the magazine into a handy locker. "Now, into your seat, and away we go."

Hermes' face brightened. "We?"

"Just an expression. I wish I *could* go with you, Hermes." Tom sighed extra heavily. "But regulations are regulations."

The waiting millions, including Dr. Zimmerman and Senator Milburn, didn't have long to wait. In the very next instant, a bolt of lightning hit the top of *Stardust One*. Almost at once, the lift-off rockets ignited. A burst of flame, and the holding brackets fell away. *Stardust One* rose — with Tom flung into the pilot's seat and Hermes piled up on the floor.

In the control room, all the men who'd gathered to watch the closed circuit TV rushed to their stations. They knew a premature launching when they saw one! Dr. Zimmerman, almost in shock, gazed at the TV screen. "Hermes, is that you?"

Tom, his face pulled oddly out of shape by the tug of gravity, managed to reply, "It's me, Dr. Zimmerman."

13

Dr. Zimmerman did his best to remain calm. "Trimble — get out of the picture. You look awful. How's Hermes?"

"I think he's broken — if not *smashed*. Dr. Zimmerman, you've *got* to get me out of here."

In all fairness to the scientist, Zimmerman *did* want to answer, "Wish I *could*, Tom." But with Senator Milburn and next year's budget on his mind, he chose his next words carefully. "Impossible, Trimble. We can't abort this mission. Now, Tom, make yourself comfortable."

"For thirty years?"

"It won't seem that long to you. Ten, at the outside. You'll find plenty of food in the storage locker. The Tang is on the top shelf behind the cracker concentrate, and — "

"Please! Dr. Zimmerman, *I'm not a trained astronaut!* I have acrophobia. You know that. I never even kept my office door closed. And — and *this is getting worse every minute!*"

"Relax, Trimble! Relax — or we can't get true readings on you." He snapped his fingers at his aide. "Quickly — some calming music for Mr. Trimble."

Unfortunately, the next sound to reach Tom's ears was a voice merrily singing, "Toot, Toot, Tootsie, Good-bye."

Dr. Zimmerman halted *that* selection.

"These things happen, Trimble," he said, "and we might as well make the best of it. And, oh! Something else. When you get back there'll be a little surprise in your pay envelope. And Trimble, your job — *First* Assistant Concept Design Engineer. How does that sound?"

"Like an award you'll present to my parents," Tom groaned.

"Hmmm. Well — I have to go. Walter and Barbara are both on the line and the President wants to congratulate me. One more thing — if you find a planet that's practical for a landing, put down and look it over. That's all." He flipped the switch. The TV screen went blank.

It would have given Tom Trimble little pleasure to have heard Senator Milburn say that he wished to congratulate "the young man who built the robot." Or to hear Dr. Zimmerman say, "I'll see that he gets the message. He's going to be out of town for a while."

But new troubles were starting. *Stardust One* was leaving Earth's gravity. Along with the helpless Hermes, Tom began floating airily about the spaceship's cabin. Using all his power, he began a swimmer's sidestroke. Slowly, slowly, he "swam" his way to the window.

What he saw was so shocking, he forgot everything but what might happen next. In one direction, Earth seemed to be rotating like a library globe. And in the other direction, the moon, big and white, was growing bigger and whiter. *"Hermes!"* he cried desperately. "We've got to get this thing *down*. *Do* something. Do what you were programmed to do!"

Hermes floated within reach and Tom grabbed a limp wrist. "Hermes, pull yourself together! That's an *order!*"

Like a rowboat stretched out from an anchor rope, Hermes drifted full-length. The sight brought Tom to his senses. "Sorry, Hermes! It's not your fault. Probably your head got bumped when you fell, and your timing pulse staticizer got jammed by your radix. But it's nothing that a screwdriver and a soldering iron can't fix. You just wait."

Using a wall as a shove-off point, Tom sailed across the cabin — too hard. He hit the other wall, hands outspread. Not only did he hit the wall, he hit a big panel of buttons marked *Vernier Thruster* and also brushed against another set of ten buttons.

Right away a whining noise began and Tom realized the engines were speeding up. The whine took on a higher and higher pitch. *Stardust One* began to tilt.

Desperately, Tom tried to slow things down. Alas! *Whiz! Whiz!* The spaceship began orbiting Earth so fast that the sun seemed to be blinking off and on like a neon sign over a restaurant.

Faster and faster! "We're reaching *relativistic* speed!" Tom groaned. "Are we getting way ahead of Earth time? Or are we racing *backwards*? Is it already next Christmas at the Cape? Or" — he gulped — "hasn't *last* Christmas come yet?"

Frantically he swam and drifted his way slowly toward the control console. "Not that I'll know what I'm doing when I get there," he told his knocked-out companion. "But *anything's* better than this."

3

Not even the demanding Dr. Zimmerman could have expected Tom Trimble to turn in an AOK kind of mission in *Stardust One*. He was not too surprised at the odd reports coming in from the down-range stations. And when *Stardust One* finally zipped off the electronic communications systems, he put everyone's mind at rest by saying that the next expected report from the spaceship would be in thirty years.

Gradually, even Tom lost interest in where he was or where he was going. The heavenly scenery that he kept passing *and* passing grew quite boring. "See one star and you've seen 'em all," he told the invalid Hermes grumpily.

Hermes was far from being his old self, although Tom was using every spare moment to check out his companion's interior. "It's just a matter of time before I get you back on your feet," he told Hermes during one of his patient's brief lucid intervals. "And the day I do, *we're* heading this buggy back to the barn!"

But the day came when one special planet, shining like a blue star in space, caught Tom's attention. And after whizzing around it several times, he decided to try for a landing. "I've *got* to stretch my legs," he said. "And that planet looks like just the place to do it." Suddenly he gasped and clutched Hermes' arm. "I can see streams and meadows! It must have an atmosphere like Earth's. I *think* I just saw a — a *castle!*"

Unexpectedly, Hermes spoke. Though his voice was groggy, he was certainly making sense. "Tom — I'll help put her down."

A goodly distance from the castle that Tom had spotted far below, Alisande, a beautiful goose girl, was on the run. She was desperately trying to escape from the wicked knight, Sir Mordred. Under her arm she held a large gander, and this extra weight made running even harder. Finally, exhausted, she dropped behind a large rock and rested her head on its hard surface.

Even though her face was smudged and her dress torn and dirty, she was plainly a runaway whom anyone would like to catch up with. After a few deep breaths she reached in her pocket for some corn kernels and sat up. "Here, Father," she said tenderly to the gander. "Eat. You must keep up your strength."

Sandy (short for Alisande) gave the bird all the kernels, even though she was terribly hungry herself. Nothing, she felt, was too good for this gander. Nothing could make up for what Sir Mordred had done to him. Though a member of King Arthur's respected Knights of the Round Table, the evil knight had put a spell on her beloved father — and turned him into a *goose*!

It mattered little that Father could only *honk* now, or that he'd sprouted white feathers and waddled when he walked. Until she could arrange to have Father changed back to his old self, she'd love him — same as always.

Sandy cuddled the gander under her arm and settled herself for a brief nap. "We'll rest here, Father. Then we'll hurry on to Camelot and seek King Arthur's help. Sir Mordred is bound to give up the chase sooner or later." She closed her eyes.

Up in *Stardust One*, Hermes was not having an easy time with the controls. "I hate to say it, Tom, but you've certainly messed up these instruments. If we make it safely to that planet I'll have to give them a good going over before we can hope to return to Earth."

An odd look came over Tom's face. "Hermes," he said slowly, "I just realized — we're back in a field of gravity. Do you suppose it could be Earth's gravity?"

Hermes shrugged. "Tom — all planets have gravity. Don't get your hopes up."

"I'm betting it's Planet Earth," Tom said stubbornly. "After all, I saw fields and streams and a castle. That would mean people, wouldn't it?"

"Maybe little green men," Hermes said ominously.

Tom suddenly chuckled. "All my life I've heard about the little green men. It just struck me — " He paused.

"What struck you?" Hermes asked, fiddling with the controls.

"That I never heard anything about little green *women*. Anyhow, I'll run over to the castle and ask to use their phone. I'll tell Zimmerman where we are. It isn't Florida, that's for sure."

Hermes shrugged. "Just one thing, Tom — in case it *isn't* Earth, better do your run to the castle in the space suit. The atmosphere may not be tolerable for Earthlings.

And *don't* hop around. That place may have a very weak gravitational pull. I'd hate to lose you now."

Tom agreed. "Okay. No hopping."

"Excuse me now. Don't talk, please. I'm going to set her down."

A loud snap of a twig awakened Sandy. She jumped to her feet. "Father! We must not tarry too long."

Father jumped into her arms and Sandy sped toward a dense thicket for safety. Safety? She ran straight into the arms of Clarence, page boy to the dreaded Sir Mordred! "Aha!" he exclaimed triumphantly and, flinging his page-boy's hairdo back, he grabbed her tight.

Sandy battled him with her one free hand. "Stop it!" she cried. "You're crushing Father."

Father set up a wild honking. To quiet him Sandy stopped struggling. "Let us go. *Please*," she begged.

"Sorry," Clarence grinned. "You belong to Sir Mordred."

"I'd rather be dead!" Sandy exclaimed. "Please, Clarence. I beg of you. If you'll only let us go, I'll be grateful forever after."

Clarence was not used to having beautiful girls beg of him. A wicked twinkle sprang into his eyes. "Perhaps you're right, Sandy. Put that silly gander down and — "

Kaboom! Stardust One crashed the sound barrier. Clarence dived for the underbrush. "What was *that*?" he asked, peeking out fearfully.

Whatever it was, Sandy was thankful for it. "It was a shooting star," she said quickly, dumping Father on the grass. "Close your eyes and make a wish, Clarence."

"Easy!" Clarence squeezed his eyelids tight. Like a flash, Sandy picked up a stone and bopped Sir Mordred's page on his pageboy hairdo. It sent him straight to slumberland.

Father honked loudly and disapprovingly. For the first time, Sandy spoke harshly to him. "Can't you understand what would happen to us if I *hadn't* crowned him!" she said angrily. "Come!"

Taking up the gander again, she hurried on, heading for woods in the distance.

Along the way she passed a pleasant little pond. Father honked. "I know. You want a swim," said Sandy. "Very well. We'll spend the night right here, then get an early start for Camelot in the morning."

There was still plenty of daylight for Father to enjoy a swim, plus a pleasant wade in the mud in search of something other than corn kernels. Sandy, using the pond as a mirror, washed her smudged face and combed her hair, and tried to arrange her dress so the rips didn't show. "How refreshing," she murmured. And, leaning back against a tree trunk, she began humming a current smash hit — "Blue Sleeves," much hummed by the folks in Camelot.

But not for long! Suddenly her eyes grew wide with fear. "Father!" she cried out. "Look! Up in the sky. It's a bird."

Father glanced briefly at *Stardust One*. As the bird was not a goose, he lost interest and went back to his muddy supper. It didn't seem to bother him a bit that the skies were filled with a tremendous roaring sound. Hermes had turned on the forward jets to ease the contact of *Stardust One* with the planet's surface.

Sandy could scarcely hear her own voice when she cried out, "Father, it's *not* a bird!"

Stardust One came closer and closer. "It's after *us*!" Sandy gasped. She snatched up Father and hid behind a fallen tree trunk.

Father, taken away from his evening meal, honked irritably.

"Shhhh. It'll hear you," Sandy whispered.

The terrible noise stopped. Sandy peeped over the log. The door of the spaceship opened and the hydraulically operated ramp unfolded. It made a couple of side-to-side movements in an automatic check of the surface.

Sandy frowned. "Now why would It stick Its tongue out at us?"

As she spoke, the "tongue" turned into steps. Father honked loudly and unpleasantly.

"Hush, dear! It's nothing to worry about, Father. Probably just some monster that flies and lives off — *people!*" Scared to death she ducked down, then dared another peek. "Oh, the Saints preserve us!" she gasped.

Down the steps of *Stardust One* came Tom. His space suit was dazzling white and his golden helmet flashed in the sun's rays.

"It isn't a snowman," Sandy muttered. "They never have gold heads. Besides, It isn't melting."

In the heavy space suit, Tom *felt* he was melting. He turned the dial of the space suit to air condition and stepped down, breathing heavily and looking from left to right.

"Don't honk a word," Sandy pleaded to Father. "Maybe he hasn't seen us."

Alas! Father had his own ideas on the subject. He honked wildly and Tom whirled in their direction.

"Now you've done it! Fly for your life!" With a mighty shove she launched Father into the air.

The frightened gander, squawking and

flapping, made for the nearest perch —Tom's helmet. Sandy dashed from her hiding place. "Oh, please!" she cried out. "Take *me* instead!"

Tom stared through his bubble visor. "Take you? Lady, you wouldn't believe what I've been through! Please — will you just tell me where I am?"

Sandy's knees knocked together. "You am in — I mean, you *are* in Rodney on Trent, Langdale Walk, Bennington Green, Devonshire Cream, Cornwall, England —Monster."

For a moment Tom thought she was calling him "Monsieur," but then, after all, Devonshire Cream didn't sound too French — and she *had* said "England."

He thought a moment. *"When* is it?"

"When?" Sandy, too, thought a moment. "Well, it's the Year of Our Lord, 508." She paused. "Why would a monster care about knowing that?"

Sandy's answer about the date made Tom forget to ask why she'd called him a monster. "Five hundred and eight! Say! The clock *can* be turned back! Albert Einstein, you really knew your stuff!" He looked around for the castle he'd seen from the skies. "Some way I've got to get *Stardust One* in orbit again and get back to the Cape."

"Cape?" Sandy was about to ask, "Whose

cape?" Instead, she curtsied. "Well, I guess we'll be on our way, Monster."

Tom looked at her. "Why do you keep calling me 'monster'?"

"Well — " Sandy hesitated. "You have no face, no ears, and you speak out of that thing in your stomach."

"That's an atmospheric communication speaker."

Sandy reached up for Father, still perched on Tom's helmet. "Did you hear that, Father? That's an — an — "

Tom patted his headgear. "If you'll help me off with this thing, you'll see what I'm like."

Sandy backed away. "Thank you," she said politely. "I really don't care to view your inside. Please. Can we go now?" Again she reached out for Father.

Tom sighed. "Where's the nearest town?"

"Camelot. It is four leagues from here. I'm going there to see someone very important in King Arthur's court about Father."

"May I ask your name, please?"

"I am Maid Alisande — Alisande Watkins, Monster."

From the spaceship Hermes watched his inventor begin to trudge off with a very pretty girl. And from a distant hillock, Sir Mordred and Clarence looked down at Sandy and Tom.

"What's she consorting with?" Sir Mordred asked.

"It's too big for a troll," his page replied. "Yet I cannot name it, Sir Mordred."

"Hmm. It seems not to have a taste for fowl. The gander seems quite safe from it." He leveled his trusty lance. "We shall see." He spurred his horse forward.

Tom more or less plunked along in his heavy outfit as Sandy tripped daintily at his side. "Are you certain you want to show yourself at the castle?" she asked. "They are not always friendly to monst — strangers."

"Look," Tom said earnestly. "Maybe at Camelot I can find a reasonable person who doesn't think I'm some creature from outer space. I mean — "

"And where *do* you come from?" asked a deep voice.

Sandy whirled around, terrified. "Sir Mordred!" she gasped.

Sir Mordred poked Tom experimentally with his lance.

Tom backed off. "Easy with the stick, friend," he said, rubbing his shoulder.

"Aiding fugitives is punishable by death," Sir Mordred said sternly.

"I'm trying to aid *myself*," Tom snapped. "Any law against that in this — er — *realm*?"

"You're my prisoner," Sir Mordred replied.

"*Both* of you. Lead on, prisoners. To Camelot!" He waved his lance menacingly.

"All *three* of us," Sandy said with spirit, clutching Father. She glanced at Tom with some disappointment. He was not living up to her idea of a really *great* monster. He hadn't even said anything through his stomach that scared Sir Mordred.

But the monster *was* polite. He gallantly carried Father in his arms. Luckily it was growing cooler as evening shadows stretched across their path.

"Is Father getting heavy?" Sandy asked timidly.

"No. Father is as light as a feather," Tom replied. He glanced back to make sure Sir Mordred on horseback was not close enough to hear them talking. "You were telling me about Father. Do go on with your story."

"Well, Sir Mordred wanted Father's land, but Father wouldn't give it up. He believes that every freeman should own the land he works." She patted the gander. "Isn't that right, Father?"

"Get to the part where Father becomes a goose," Tom urged.

"Gander."

"Okay, gander."

"Well, when I returned from the Haymarket, the gander was in Father's chair finishing Father's breakfast."

Tom plodded onward. "So naturally you figured it was your old man transformed by some evil spell."

"Certainly. What else could it have been? Father, as I remember him, was nowhere to be seen and the door was latched. If only I could see Merlin! I know he could make Father himself again."

"Merlin the Magician?"

Sandy nearly stopped walking. "*You* know Merlin?"

"Just by reputation."

"Oh. He is known beyond Camelot?"

"Far beyond," Tom answered briefly.

"Well, shortly after all that happened, Sir Mordred rode up to the pond where I'd taken Father for an outing. He said I was his prisoner. I made it very clear that I was the daughter of Watkins, the Woodcarver, a freeman. But Sir Mordred demanded proof."

"And you couldn't prove it?" Tom asked.

"How could I? Father really couldn't help me. He could only honk. Anyhow, Sir Mordred laid claim to me."

"Along with your father's property?"

"No. That's the *strangest* thing. He has yet to proclaim our land as his own. Now I don't know what to do. I can't leave Father like this. He'd fall prey to some fox."

Tom glanced back once again at Sir Mordred. "And there's the fox," he muttered.

4

Tom's first close glimpse of Camelot made him feel glad that, if he *did* have to go backward in time, he'd landed in such a pretty place. Sunset light turned the castle's towers and turrets to rich gold — just the sort of home Tom expected King Arthur to own.

As they entered the courtyard through the big gateway, servants were careful to keep a good distance away from the strange visitor. Tom realized that he must be an odd and frightening sight to these people of the year 508.

In the main hall of the castle, flickering torches gave the room the look of a huge, dim cavern. The tapestries that hung along the bleak stone walls made this part of King Arthur's castle a little more cheerful. And the knights and their ladies seated around a huge, heavily laden dining table were certainly in a cheerful mood.

King Arthur, at the head of the table, was also enjoying his dinner party. He lifted a goblet of mead. "And now," he announced, "Merlin has promised another of his astonishing entertainments. Merlin, do step forward."

Some of the guests stirred a little uneasily. Sometimes Merlin the Magician's performances were a little frightening. But as he was King Arthur's number one man, the guests all clapped loudly.

Robed in black, Merlin loomed darkly against the light of the flaring torches. Before him was a shallow bowl of burning oil. He waved long, thin fingers over it and spoke in a chilling voice. "I will now transform an ordinary mouse into a glass of wine and then *drink* it."

Several of the knights' ladies raised their dainty slippers off the stone floor. A mouse could be hiding *anywhere* in the castle.

Sir Gawain, Knight First Class, was nervous, too. If ever there was a brave, square-shooting knight, Sir Gawain was that. But he sensed that Merlin did not care at all for square-shooting types like himself. It was Merlin who had sneeringly nicknamed him Sir

Gawain the Square. So it was not the mouse-about-to-be-wine that spooked Sir Gawain, but Merlin the Mouse-Changer. Nervously he threw a roast beef bone across the room.

For a moment King Arthur's dogs set up a noisy row for this delicacy.

"Sir Gawain," Merlin sneered — as usual. "If I were to turn you to stone, perhaps I could continue?"

Everybody laughed wildly at this clever remark. Even Sir Gawain managed a faint smile, and Merlin proceeded with his mouse trick.

Fortunately, Sandy and Tom missed his entire unpleasant performance. But as they waited at the entrance with Sir Mordred, they could hear the standing ovation from the Let's-Hear-it-for-Merlin faction. Sandy and Father-the-goose were led away. Sir Mordred poked his lance against Tom's suit. "Move," he said roughly. Then he turned to his page. "Clarence," he said, "you know where to take the Maid Alisande. See that she remains there."

Merlin stepped out from the main hall just as Sir Mordred finished his instructions. "What have you brought us this time, Sir Mordred? Man or beast?" he asked.

Sir Mordred bowed. "I'm told It flies, but I see no wings."

"Will It fetch a ransom?"

"I can't imagine who'd pay to get him back. But he's certain to prove *entertaining*."

"Haw! Haw!"

Something told Tom that he was overhearing two scalawags talking. They had *some* secret between them, he was certain.

Sir Mordred lowered his voice. "Has our poacher confessed his crime against the Crown?"

"He has not! He still refuses to admit guilt."

"Ah, well," Mordred sighed. "Tomorrow will bring fresh thoughts on the problem. Right now I am eager to display today's bag for the King."

"And what of your *baggage*?" Merlin leered and winked.

If Tom remembered his Knights of the Round Table correctly, "baggage" referred to a *girl*, not a suitcase.

"Safe enough," Mordred grinned. "Safe here," he added.

Merlin's face clouded. His voice became stern. "Here! Mordred! We cannot have that deluded girl wandering the halls of Camelot. You go too far!"

Sir Mordred grinned wickedly. "*She* won't go far, Merlin."

"Merlin?" Tom asked. "Merlin the Magician? Say! You're the guy Sandy's looking for. She thinks her father's been zapped into a goose and that you can do a little of that abra-cadabra stuff and make everything okay again."

"*Abra-cadabra stuff!*" Merlin cried out at this insult to his image. "A hex on you! You have seen your last sunset!" He stalked off.

"Does he mean that?" Tom asked.

"If he doesn't, I do," Sir Mordred replied, giving Tom a rough shove. "Forward."

"Sir Mordred the Dauntless and his Monster," a servant called out loudly as the pair entered the main hall.

Ladies shrieked and flung themselves on any handy knight.

"Fear not. I have It subdued," the Dauntless One explained. He bowed to the king. "Your Majesty!"

Tom moved forward quickly. "King Arthur — may I have a few minutes with you?"

Several knights leaped to their feet, ready to protect their king. Sir Mordred pushed forward. "Your Highness, this creature, and five others like him, set upon me in the forest with firebrands and lances. I slew the others but spared this one as a curio for Your Highness."

Tom was about to burst right out of his golden helmet at this out-and-out untrue report. He gasped, "Why, you — you — "

But King Arthur merely gazed calmly at Senator Milburn's "fine young American."

"Hmmm. The head *is* most unusual. Would you say It is a land animal?"

Tom spoke straight from the heart although those present would have sworn he spoke straight from the stomach. "It's this space suit, your honor. In slacks and a two-button blazer I'd look just like — " he gulped.

"Sir Mordred," asked His Majesty, "what are your plans for the thing? It's hardly large enough for a beast of burden. It's too big for a pet. And what does It eat? For that matter *where* does It eat?"

Sir Mordred answered quickly, "I don't wish to frighten the ladies present, Sire. But I'll just say It would be *dangerous* to keep about."

Gentle Sir Gawain shuddered — not at the thought of being devoured, but by his good guess that Sir Mordred had an unpleasant fate planned for this strange creature. And if there was anything Sir Gawain the Square hated it was an unpleasant fate — for *any-thing*. He spoke up bravely. "Your High-ness, It might be trained to be useful in some way."

"Useful!" Tom exploded. "I'm a Valley U.

graduate and an *expert* computer designer. I'm *already* useful."

Sir Mordred gave him a warning punch on the arm. "I'm thinking more along the lines of a burning, Your Highness. It's been quite a while since we've had one, Your Highness. What say you, Sire?"

"Burning!" Tom gasped. "Burning what?"

"Silence!" the Dauntless One thundered. "Silence, or I'll cleave you where you stand."

King Arthur raised his hand. "Not at the banquet table, please. But I must say that burning is fit punishment for the crime of attacking a Round Table Knight." He looked keenly at Mordred. "I also must say you seem to get more than your share of attacks and encounters with poachers. I trust there is no evil afoot in the name of knight errantry?"

Merlin, who had been absent while stowing away his mouse for a wine show at some later date, came back into the hall. He bowed extra deeply to the king — an act which his Highness found very pleasing.

King Arthur smiled at both his powerful Magician and his dauntless Mordred. "Very well, then. A burning at prime meridian tomorrow."

"High noon!" Tom exclaimed. "Now *wait a minute*. When do I get my time at bat? I mean — don't you want to hear the other side of the story?"

As the king hesitated, Merlin hurriedly said, "It is late, Your Majesty."

"Fair's fair, Merlin." King Arthur turned to Tom. "Very well. Speak, Thing. I wouldst know something of your clan — or do you travel in packs?"

Tom tugged at his helmet. "I think I could answer questions better if I could get this helmet off. Do you have a wrench around here?"

King Arthur frowned. *Wench?* It was hard for him to see what a maid could do here. He asked Tom, "How could a wench help you?"

"To get this helmet off."

"Very well," said the king. "Bring in Peg, the kitchen wench."

Tom thought that stout Peg was certainly a very unusual *wrench*, but he made the best of the situation. He tapped his helmet. "Give it a good twist to the left."

The entire court gasped as The Thing's head came off in Peg's arms. And when a second head came into view, even Peg the Wench backed off in fright.

"Probably a temperature change caused the threads to expand," Tom explained, rubbing his head.

"I know nothing of such threads," said the King. "Get on with it. Speak."

Suddenly, Tom had the feeling he would have been better off traveling to Alpha Centauri. At least from there he'd have a chance of getting back to twentieth-century Planet Earth in *thirty* years. Now it looked as though it would take a bit over *fourteen hundred* years on Planet Earth just to catch up.

"There was once a great man named Albert Einstein," Tom began slowly. "He discovered a lot about time."

King Arthur was certainly fair. He showed it by doing his best to keep awake as Tom desperately tried to explain that His Highness's future had already passed.

"Now, then," Tom struggled on, "you'll recall my explanation of the law of gravity and how this theory is applied to orbiting objects!"

"Cease!" Merlin thundered. Although he was a science-fiction fan himself, he could stand no more.

All the knights and ladies jerked awake and the royal dogs set up a loud barking. Tom could scarcely hear his own voice. "It happened just the way I told you. I swear. That is — it *will* happen that way."

"Why, then, are you not fourteen hundred

years old?" asked the king reasonably, as the hubbub died down.

"It's difficult to explain, Your Highness."

"It certainly is — I mean, was," sighed King Arthur. "Take him away, Sir Mordred." He added, almost sadly, "To the dungeon."

Guards stepped forward. With their help, Sir Mordred had no trouble in getting the luckless Tom Trimble out of the banquet hall. But in the dimly lit corridor they nearly knocked over a castle page standing in the shadows.

"Watch where you're going, varlet, lest we take you to the dungeon too!" Sir Mordred bellowed.

The page, Maid Sandy Watkins, disguised in Clarence's clothes, stepped back against the wall. She hid in the dark shadows and awaited Sir Mordred's return journey. She was soon rewarded by sounds of heavy footsteps — plus a little inside information.

"Prime meridian," the Dauntless One chuckled. "Tomorrow! It'll be the best show Camelot's ever had! No one should miss seeing the monster go up in smoke!"

Sandy gulped. "There is only one monster in town," she muttered. "That means *him*! And where there's smoke there's — " she shuddered. "*Fire!* Oh, no! I must help him. He was *very* kind to Father."

Off she sped to the room where she'd left Clarence. "Thank goodness!" she exclaimed as she entered. "He still sleeps peacefully. Lucky for me I found a hammer to cause such sweet rest!"

She picked up the food basket intended for Sir Mordred's late-evening snack, and, pausing only to tuck in the hammer, hurried out the door.

5

Smoky flaring torches made the dungeon's black shadows leap and stretch along the damp stone walls. "Who goes?" a guard cried out.

"Food for Sir Mordred's prisoner," Sandy answered, making her voice gruff.

The guard pointed farther along in the shadows. "Down there."

Sandy caught her breath as she neared the terrible room. "I never knew Camelot was like *this*!" Prisoners, some sleeping, some scratching, some coughing, were chained here and there.

Over in a corner was the latest addition to this unhappy group. Tom, also chained, his space helmet beside him, looked up. Not even Clarence's clothes fooled Tom. "Over here, Sandy," he said quietly.

Sandy picked her way through the gloom. She dropped down beside Tom. "Oh, Thing, I hardly recognized you without your regular head," she whispered.

"Will you *stop* that, Sandy? This is getting serious. I get burned at the stake tomorrow."

Sandy nodded. "Prime meridian," she said sadly. "I heard."

"Can you believe it? Me! *Burned at the stake?*"

"It's such a blessing," she said softly.

"Blessing!"

"Witches and warlocks get stoned to death," his only friend in Camelot replied. "But see! I've brought you something." She lifted the food basket.

"Not Father, surely," Tom gasped.

"Oh, *no*. Father's enjoying a swim in the cistern right now. I brought you a hammer to free you from your chains."

Tom sighed. "Thanks, Sandy. But it wouldn't work."

"It worked on Clarence," Sandy replied calmly.

Tom stared. "Your mean you bopped Clarence to save me?"

"Bopped?"

"Forget it, Sandy. Tell me — why have you taken such a risk just to help a — *monster*?"

Sandy thought it over. "Well — you have harmed no one. You were kind to Father. I believe you should be set free to return to your natural habitat."

Tom sighed. "If I couldn't convince King Arthur, I guess I couldn't make you believe what my natural habitat is. But, Sandy — do I really look like a monster to you?"

Sandy looked at him carefully. "Not as much with your outside head off. But you *did* when you came out of your shell breathing smoke."

"That was *steam*. It was hot as an oven in that capsule when we reentered."

Sandy paid no attention to such words as "capsule" or "reentered." "Hot as an *oven!*" she exclaimed. "That's what I mean! How does an ordinary man live in an oven?"

Tom started to explain a few twentieth-century marvels such as space-suit material and air conditioning, but he suddenly stopped. "Here — I'll show you." Turning a control dial on his space suit, cool air ballooned his shape. "You see — what's the matter, Sandy?"

"No! No!" she whispered as she watched him grow fatter.

"Don't be scared. Wait. I'll show you something else. Got a match?"

"It isn't settled," Sandy blushed. "But Father's been wanting me to marry Timothy the Potter."

Tom might have groaned loudly if a sudden wonderful idea hadn't hit him. "The burning! What have I been worrying about? Sandy, I'll be okay at the stake! You watch and see!"

It was all Sandy could stand. She backed away in terror.

"Come back, Sandy! I'm not any different from you!"

But Maid Sandy vanished into the gloom. Tom, leaping after her, was jerked right off his feet by the chain.

From the next cell came the sound of a loud groan. Carefully Tom stood up and peered through the barred window just above his head. He could only dimly see another prisoner. "You all right?" he called in a low voice.

"Who asks such a stupid question?" came the answer, along with a second groan.

"My name's Tom Trimble. I'm Sir Mordred's prisoner."

"Mordred! You mean *Satan* himself. He wants me to confess to killing one of his deer."

"Why not just say you did and get out?"

"If I confess I must forfeit all my properties to him. It is a cruel and unjust law."

"Well, you can't take it with you. And you do look as though you're in bad shape."

Groan and silence. Then:

"My land is my only legacy to my beloved daughter, Alisande. She will have nothing if I admit guilt."

"Alisande! Is your name 'Watkins'? Are you Sandy's father?"

"You know my daughter! Tell me, is she well and safe from harm?"

"Fine, fine," Tom said soothingly.

"The poor child must think me dead," said Sandy's father, sadly.

"Actually, she thinks you are a goose."

"A *goose*! Her own father?"

"I meant — a gander," Tom replied.

Sandy's father groaned again. "It matters not how she feels about me. She must get word to King Arthur — must tell him Sir Mordred is using this evil trick to steal land from a freeman."

"I figured it was a land grab." Tom nodded. "What about this guy Merlin? Is he a kind of partner?"

"They may be in league. Both are ambitious men and soon will have enough land and vassals to be a threat to our King."

"Don't you worry, Mr. Watkins. Soon as I'm through being burned at the stake, I'll spill the whole deal."

There was such a long pause that Tom began to worry that Mr. Watkins was no more. Then he heard a weak voice. "Would it not show more foresight to tell him before the burning?"

Sir Mordred couldn't have chosen a better day for the burning. For one thing, there was no threat of rain.

All of Camelot had turned out for the event and there was an air of special holiday as minstrels strolled through the crowds and vendors set up their stands for selling refreshing goblets of honey-flavored mead to the thirsty spectators.

Sir Mordred, wearing a new suit of black chain mail, looked on the scene with great satisfaction. But Merlin was not in such a good mood. "It alarms me, Mordred, that you have let the entire night pass without successfully capturing that silly young Alisande."

Sir Mordred frowned. "Fear not. At this very moment, my page boy seeks her out. When found, you may be sure there'll be no escape for her. Ah! Here comes our King."

King Arthur walked directly to the royal box, Sir Gawain at his side. "I had troubling dreams last night, Knight," he said, seating himself. "All those strange tales we heard kept popping into my head. Was it the Wright Brothers who discovered radio?"

"I think not, Your Highness." Sir Gawain bowed. "That was Babe Ruth — or some such name. I must admit I dozed off now and then. But I'm still wondering — couldn't the thing be trained as Court Jester? It tells the best lies we've ever heard. Better even than Sir Mordred's."

"How's that, Sir Gawain?" asked Mordred.

Sir Gawain the Square was spared the need to reply as a roar from the crowd signaled the entrance of Tom Trimble. Wearing his gloves, helmet, and puffed-out air-conditioned space suit, Tom looked every inch a monster — an *enormous* monster. Beside him, the black-hooded executioners seemed puny. But they marched him past the cheering, jeering spectators and past King Arthur's royal box before leading him to the stake.

From her hiding place in the bushes, Maid Sandy watched as Tom's wrists were tied to the stake with leather thongs. "Oh, Father, It is most brave, isn't It?"

Tom stood proudly. "King Arthur," he called. "I'd like a word with Your Highness after the burning."

Sir Mordred and Merlin exchanged uneasy glances, and King Arthur stared in astonishment. He shrugged. "If It feels up to it, I see no harm," he told his staff. "It seems to have grown greatly overnight, though." He nodded toward Tom. "Very well."

"Make sure It is bound securely," Sir Mordred shouted.

Up until that moment Tom wasn't worrying. In fact, he could hardly wait to see the dazzled looks of all Camelot when the last faggot had burned to an ember and he would stride out unharmed. "Fire away," he said cheerfully.

And then it happened! In testing the thongs, one of the executioners bumped the cooling system dial on the space suit. Very suddenly, and at the very moment the fire around his boots was lighted, Tom looked as though he'd gone on a crash diet.

As the flames leaped high, the crowd cheered. Only Sandy could not bear to look. "I know It is not handsome, Father. Yet It must be a mortal man. Why else would I have this strange feeling for him — It, I mean?"

Tom was having a strange feeling himself — a rather rare-to-medium feeling. But the fire that could not penetrate the space-suit material burned through the thongs. And just as Tom was beginning to go from medium to well-done, he felt his arms drop free. He hastily stepped out from the flames. A moan of awe swept the crowd.

As this sound was better than cheers to Tom Trimble, he paced forward to sweep a deep bow to King Arthur. Unfortunately, this brave performance was ruined. Smoking pants ruined it. *Eeeeyoowe!*

Even Sir Mordred the Dauntless took a backwards step at this display of ferocity. Tom promptly headed for the castle entrance. The crowd willingly made a broad path for this muttering, mad monster, and Tom disappeared into the cool dimness of King Arthur's royal residence.

Once inside he hot-footed it down the corridor. "I've got to find Father! Where there's Father there'll be a cistern. And do I need a *swim*!"

Outside, King Arthur, the knights, and Merlin all knew something must be done. "We can't have It roaming the halls of Camelot," said the King. "Mordred — it was all your doing."

"And I shall be the Thing's *undoing*," Mordred swore. He turned and shouted to the crowd. "There is nothing to fear! What fire can't do, cold steel will." He turned to Clarence. "Don't fail my order *this* time, Page. Go back inside and fetch me my sword!"

Clarence dropped to his knees. "Me? Go in where the monster roams? Oh, sire!"

Mordred jerked Clarence to his feet. "Thou

art on thin ice as it is, Page. I bid thee obey."
His voice dropped to a whisper. "And then go
find the *other* roamer this time. *You know
who I mean.*"

Sandy, still in the bushes, whispered, too,
to Father. "I must go to his — I mean
Its — aid. Oh, dear!" Quickly she scampered,
fast as possible with Father in her arms, to
the servant's entrance. "I'll drop you off in
the cistern, Father."

No sooner did she have Father safely afloat
than she smashed square into Clarence.
"*Oh!*"

"You're in bad trouble," he said. "Sir
Mordred's looking for you. I'll get you right
after I get Sir Mordred's sword. He's going to
take care of the monster first, and you next."

"Oh, Clarence!" Sandy pleaded. "Can we
not declare king's truce for a bit? We must
help the monster. My heart tells me he's a
man, not an *It*."

No sooner had she uttered this plea than
Father seemed to rise straight up from the
water. He honked in alarm as he tried to get a
firm perch on a rising golden helmet. And
Tom, looking like a high-ranking officer with
a wingéd bird atop his helmet, came blub-
blubbing upward. "I can explain everything,"
he gurgled.

"There's no time!" Sandy exclaimed. "Clarence is to get Sire Mordred's sword. That villain means to run you through."

"And he's the best swordsman in all of England," Clarence added with pride.

"So I remember," Tom said gloomily. "I learned it all at the Saturday afternoon movies."

"Cease this idle talk," Sandy begged. "You must defend yourself in *some* way. Can you bite?"

Tom didn't bother to answer. He turned to Clarence. "Is there a back door? Or maybe a laundry chute?"

"None. And only the king can order the drawbridge lowered. You're stuck."

"Stuck? Never! Clarence, let us speed to the sword department. I need a choice of weapons!"

As voices in the distance were growing louder, Tom had little time to closely examine the sword rack. "I don't know a sword from a letter opener," he muttered.

"Just pick any one," Clarence said. "It matters little. You'll be killed, anyway."

"I don't like your attitude, Clarence," Tom said sternly. He moved along the display of weapons and stopped to examine the largest one of all resting in a heavy anvil.

"Excalibur!" Tom said excitedly. "Say, that's King Arthur's own sword, isn't it?"

"But you'll never be able to lift it!" Sandy cried. "Only the pure in heart — "

"I know the story," Tom interrupted. Bracing himself to pull the famous weapon free, he tugged with both hands. Excalibur lifted out easily.

"Oh, I knew it!" Sandy squealed. "Your heart *is* pure after all! Oh, I can't bear to watch!" Off she fled, leaving her pure-hearted monster to the doom that must surely follow.

6

Tom took a couple of practice slashes with the sword. "You know, Clarence, as a man of science I always did have an explanation why nobody could pull this sword out. I figured it was stuck to a *lodestone*."

Clarence had no time to ask for more detailed information. "I must deliver Sir Mordred his sword. If he thought for a moment I had befriended thee — "

"Clarence, I *need* your help."

"Impossible!" Clarence gasped. "Sir Mordred would boil me in oil!"

"He'll never know," Tom said quickly. "Just tell me, which way is north?"

Clarence shrugged helplessly. "All I can

tell you is that the sun rises over yon battlement — and sets beyond the tower."

"Great." Tom squared his shoulders east and west and faced north. "Now hand me Sir Mordred's sword."

Clarence watched nervously as Tom drew the blade from the scabbard and placed it carefully on the floor. He lined up the swordpoint exactly to face the northern direction. "Now I need a hammer. Got one? Anything heavy will do. I'm going to try to magnetize this sword."

"Magnetize?"

"A solid blow can rearrange the electrons within the atoms of steel. Give me something, *quick*!"

Clarence grabbed a war mace from the rack. "Will this do?" he asked anxiously.

The answer came as with a loud *clang*. Tom whacked down the mace. More clangs echoed as Sir Mordred bellowed from the hallway, "Page, where art thou?" He turned to King Arthur. "When Your Majesty next sends a company to fight the enemy I'd like to recommend a volunteer."

"I think I can find room for both you and your page if you bungle *this*," King Arthur said coldly.

Merlin and Sir Gawain trailed behind the pair as they reached a turn in the hallway, and all four were nearly bumped over by Clarence coming at top speed with his master's sword safely tucked in the scabbard.

"It went that way!" Clarence panted, waving his hand in the wrong direction. Too late he noticed Tom's wet footprints were clearly in view and leading to the great hall. "I mean, *that* way," he babbled.

King Arthur pushed past to the sword room. "And it appears It took *my* sword! Strange! No doubt It has taken refuge in the great hall."

"As good a place as any to carve It up!" Sir Mordred exclaimed. He started to draw his sword from the scabbard. To the amazement of all, it wouldn't budge. Sir Mordred the Dauntless was fast becoming Sir Mordred the Scarlet. "It must be rusted," he said. "I've been using my lance of late."

King Arthur stepped forward. Anybody who could lift Excalibur would have no trouble with an ordinary weapon. "Allow me," he said graciously.

But before Sir Mordred's sword could become available for action, Merlin, Sir Gawain, Sir Mordred, and King Arthur worked mightily on the problem as a foursome. With a tremendous heave at either end, the blade came free — but Merlin and Mordred tumbled flat on their backs, and His Majesty and Sir Gawain barely managed to keep their balance. Clarence wisely pretended he hadn't been looking.

The swordplay that followed in the Great Hall was nothing Sir Mordred cared to recall in later years.

Tom's footprints were easy to spot. They went straight to the tapestry-covered wall. "Hiding!" Sir Mordred exclaimed. "The coward! This will be a one-stroke-and-out affair, Your Majesty!"

Sir Mordred strode forward, grasping his sword in both hands. "Of a surety I shall cleave thee in twain," he shouted at the slight bulge behind the covered wall.

He heaved the sword back over his head for the deadly blow he planned to deal. There was a sudden *snap* as the blade fastened tight to his new chain-mail jacket. Try as he would, Sir Mordred could *not* pull it free.

Out darted Tom. He gave Sir Mordred a rather gentle poke in the stomach with Excalibur's tip. "Ooof!" the knight gasped, bending forward to clutch his middle.

Tom darted merrily to the far side of the banquet table which was set for the noonday meal. "Over there!" he called out cheerfully. Sir Mordred again sought assistance from the Camelotonians present. Clarence watched the scene with growing hope.

Sir Mordred, once again armed, came forward in a killing rage. "Thing — I'llst have thee sectioned like a beef," he bellowed. With one sweep of the sword to clear the table, Sir Mordred was again in trouble. Metal plates, metal tankards, and even some delicate metal bud vases set to mark knights' ladies places, came leaping to the blade—and stuck!

Tom dealt his opponent another pink on the chain armor. Sir Mordred turned in a fury to Sir Gawain. "Take those blasted things off my sword," he demanded.

Sir Gawain hesitated. "I don't know. Would that be the *square* thing to do? I hate to become involved."

"Remove them quickly," Sir Mordred shouted.

"Would it be fair — and square?" Sir Gawain asked the King.

"A good knight must learn to use his own judgment," His Majesty answered.

"Well — he *is* one of our own circle," Sir Gawain said, frowning. He reached for a tankard. Right away it stuck to his metal gauntlets. Tom took advantage of this unexpected plus to give Sir Mordred another jab, and Clarence, in the excitement of the moment, cheered.

"Dost thou forget the penalty for treason, Page?" Sir Mordred blasted forth.

(Above) "It's after us!" Maid Alisande is Sandy (played by Sheila White). A goose girl in King Arthur's time, she is terrified by the spaceship roaring toward her. (Below) "Why should it stick its tongue out at us?" Sandy wonders as the ship's ramp unfolds. Is that a snowman descending — or a monster?

"Why do you keep calling me 'monster'?" asks Tom Trimble (Dennis Dugan). "Well, you have no face, no ears, and you speak out of that thing in your stomach," answers Sandy.

The bad guys, Merlin the Magician (Juan Moody) and Sir Mordred (Jim Dale), plot the takeover of King Arthur's kingdom of Camelot.

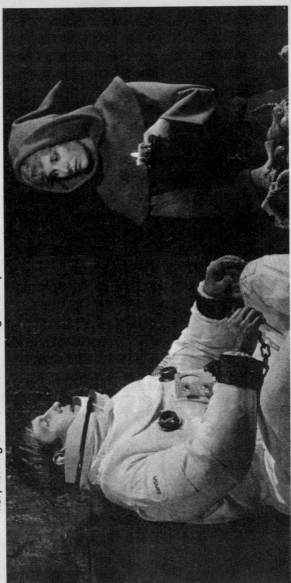

Thanks to Sir Mordred, Tom is to be burned at the stake. Here, Sandy brings Tom some food, and a hammer to break his chains. "I'll be okay," Tom tells her, turning on the air-conditioning in his space suit.

"Let the flames rise!" cries Merlin as King Arthur (Kenneth More), Sir Gawain (John Le Mesurier), and all the court look on. "King Arthur," calls Tom, "I'd like a word with you after the burning."

Tom's suit collapses but the fire burns the thongs binding him and he escapes. Here, he pulls King Arthur's sword from a magnetic stone, for an interesting duel with the armored Sir Mordred.

Tom Trimble must fight in a tournament against Sir Mordred. He knows nothing about knightly combat, so he puts his look-alike robot, Hermes, on a horse. Here, Hermes' head is knocked off by Sir Mordred's pike, but Hermes rides on.

A wide view of the tournament. King Arthur, Sir Gawain, and Merlin are in the royal box. Tom, with page Clarence (Rodney Bewes), watches from the castle.

When Merlin steals Tom's laser gun, Sir Mordred thinks they've won. But Tom, in shining armor, beats the laser beam and rides the Stardust Rover to victory.

Kissing through a plastic bubble may be strange, but Tom and Sandy really love each other.

King Arthur sighed. "The enemies of England would take heart if they could witness this."

"It is metal attracting metal!" Merlin called out. "Touch not metal with the blade!"

"Its head be not of metal," Sir Mordred yelled. With a fierce tug he pulled Sir Gawain's gauntlets right off his fellow knight's hands and made a lunge for Tom's head.

But Tom remembered all those Saturday matinee movies. He raced for the staircase, Sir Mordred a good three jumps behind him. Up, up they went, with Tom getting in a few good jabs before they reached the battlements topping the castle walls.

Tom, his back to the scenery of the Camelot countryside, dodged the mighty swings of Sir Mordred's sword and waved the gold-hilted Excalibur. And then it happened! Sir Mordred's blade once again missed Tom's head — and came down like a ton of steel on Excalibur. There it *stuck*. With a last mighty backwards heave Sir Mordred jerked His Majesty's sword from Tom's hand.

"Mordred! Mordred!" Merlin yelled from the top of the staircase. "You have It. Put an end to It!"

Sir Mordred's lips curled in a sinister smile. He had never felt such a sense of power. Armed with what had become the heaviest weapon in all England, he made his death-dealing swing. Tom dodged. And to the horror of all — even Tom — Sir Mordred went swinging right along with the weight of his combat equipment. Over the battlement he sailed. For a moment he was outlined against Camelot's blue skies. Then — nothing!

Sir Gawain paled as he gazed downward to the courtyard. Merlin glared at Tom. King Arthur took the event with his usual kingly calm. He gazed down at his fallen knight. "Sir Mordred has more lives than nine cats. He survives!" He turned to Tom. "It would seem that you are top sword around here — not an enviable position. And you, Page! There is much to be questioned in your recent behavior."

It was a stiff, sore, aching Sir Mordred who watched Clarence pounding away at the dented armor. "Enough, I say! Take it elsewhere. And when you're finished I'm having you boiled in oil for letting that wench, Maid Alisande, get away."

Clarence stood up. "I've found some dents, Sir Mordred, not included in the original estimate. It might take a few more days to complete a really first-class job."

"Just get at it," his master bellowed. "Get yourself out of my sight."

Clarence, hurrying from the room and dragging the clanking armor behind him, bumped into Merlin at the doorway. Merlin stared at Sir Mordred's battle apparel. "Is he — gone?"

"I'm still here, Merlin," Mordred called out grumpily. "And what is the topic at the Round Table?"

"Your recent defeat at the hands of this — Thing. Or whatever you prefer to call It.

"The devil's disciple is what *I* call It. See what It's done to my sword."

Merlin nodded. "Nevertheless, I'm afraid the creature has worked his way into His Majesty's good graces. Mordred, if you're to regain favor around the Round Table, you'll have to act quickly."

If Sir Mordred could have seen the personally conducted tour of the Round Table that Tom was enjoying, his headache would have grown worse.

Tom moved slowly, reading aloud the knights' names marked on the table. "Sir Lancelot. Is he in Court now?"

"On leave," said the King. "I believe something was mentioned about rescuing a maiden."

"I heard he was into that." Tom nodded. He moved along. "And here's Sir Galahad's place! Wow! Wait'll the boys at the Cape hear about this! That reminds me, Your Highness — I've got to get back there and back to the twentieth century."

King Arthur sighed. "You keep saying that, but I don't see how anyone can possibly go *back* to the twentieth *anything* when we're only in the sixth. Tell me, Thomas, and it won't go beyond this room, I promise. Just where *do* you come from?"

Tom drew a deep breath. "Well, remember I told you about Columbus sailing the ocean blue in fourteen hundred and ninety-two?"

King Arthur clapped his hands to his ears. "Please — I couldn't go through all that again. Bugs that jitter. Beatles that throw rocks."

"*Play* rock." Tom took another deep breath. "Maybe when I show you *Stardust One* you'll understand." He glanced down again at the table. "Sir Mordred's place. King, I don't like to get mixed up in local politics, but my sources tell me Mordred's got a sideline going."

"A sideline?"

"Moonlighting. He's got one poor guy in your dungeons now trying to get him to confess to poaching — which the guy never did. He's doing it so he can rip off his land."

"That's a serious charge against one of my knights, Thomas. I trust you have proof?"

"I do. In the dungeon. Follow me."

King Arthur frowned. "A king does not follow a captive . . . no matter how weird the captive."

"Sorry! After you, King."

In the dungeon there was no sign of Mr. Watkins, but the cell was not empty. A Knight of the Round Table was present—Sir Mordred!

King Arthur raised his eyebrows. "You're not exactly the person I was looking for, Sir Mordred. But as long as you're here you might as well know that I'm told you're mixed up in a — "

"Land grab," said Tom.

"Land grab," His Highness repeated.

"A blatant lie," Sir Mordred thundered. "My honor is doubted! I demand satisfaction on the field of honor!"

"*Again!*" Tom exclaimed.

King Arthur looked a bit unhappy. "You showed me no proof, Thomas. It is Sir Mordred's right — though I've lost some good knights that way."

"A joust!" Sir Mordred roared. "To the death!"

"You mean lances and horses?" Tom gasped. "King, I don't even ride English style."

It was a very sad Thomas Trimble who returned from the unexpected interview in the dungeon. "I'd better get busy on this problem," he muttered. "As they say, three times and out. *Out!* That's the answer! I've got to get out of here." He hurried off to find Clarence.

Tom's problem seemed as nothing to one who expected to be boiled in oil in the near future. Clarence hammered away at Sir Mordred's armor, adding a few new dents here and there. "You're already a goner," he said to Tom, almost absent-mindedly.

"If I don't win the joust *you'll* be a goner, Clarence. Now how about helping me out of here? Our side just might win. How about it?"

"How's our side going to win if you're out?"

"I have a plan. Can't tell you now."

Clarence thought it over. "There's a rope by the old outer chapel," he finally said. "I'll be there."

"When?"

Clarence crossed his fingers. IX.

"Good. Nine o'clock then."

Sharp on the hour Thomas Trimble went over the wall!

7

Camelot never looked livelier. Brightly striped tents were scattered around a field of green. Banners waved against a blue sky. Bleachers were filled by an excited crowd waiting for the main event to begin. And beautifully dressed ladies with their knights, also wearing their best, took their seats on either side of King Arthur's royal box.

"Here he comes!" ladies called out, thrilled to see the hometown favorite, Sir Mordred, come prancing out on a magnificent black charger. He wore his other suit of black gleaming mail, and black plumes waved from his helmet.

He guided his steed to King Arthur's front-row seat and reined up. "What news of my — er, worthy opponent, Your Highness?" he asked.

Sir Gawain spoke up. "We've searched the castle from turret to dungeon. He must have fled in the night."

"Small satisfaction for me, then." Sir Mordred scowled.

King Arthur nodded. "And even less for the crowd. If he has not made an appearance soon, we'll consider him vanquished."

Merlin leaned forward. "And with it, I trust," he said silkily, "the creature's dishonorable charges against Sir Mordred are also vanquished."

The King, about to nod, straightened high on his outdoor recreation throne. "Hello! What's this?"

A white plow horse bearing a figure resplendent in astronaut-white, with gold helmet and visor, came jogging up the jousting lane.

King Arthur did not look too pleased. "It seems you shall not have your victory without bloodletting after all, Mordred."

Actually, Sir Mordred was not too pleased, either. He scowled fiercely. "My pleasure, and let's get on with it. Let the trumpets sound!"

Nobody noticed Maid Alisande huddled off in a far corner with Father in her arms. She gazed intently at Sir Mordred's opponent.

"Oh, Father! It does look so handsome all in white with Its little red, white, and blue flag. Perhaps It is not an It, but a *he*. I find my fear has changed to fondness. Why else doth my heart beat so fast? Oh, we *must* give him something to carry into battle and his world beyond."

Swiftly she broke through the lines of onlookers and rushed up to the out-of-towner. "Oh, Thomas — it would make me so proud if you'd carry something of mine into battle —if you can call such a lopsided contest a battle. Please wear this."

Father let out a honk that might have been heard in Cape Canaveral.

"It's from Father, too," Sandy said shyly, holding out one of Father's tail feathers.

"Thank you," said — *Hermes!*

Sir Mordred did not miss this tender scene. His jaws clenched in fury. "So the wench has been here all the time. I'll deal with *her* as soon as I fix *It* — on the end of my lance!" He flipped down his visor, ready for business.

Sir Mordred was not the only one to glimpse Maid Alisande's feather presentation. Page Clarence peered through Tom's binoculars through the slotted wall opening of

Sir Mordred's room in the castle. Behind him, Tom, decked out in the same slacks, blazer, and moccasins he'd worn on lift-off, was examining Sir Mordred's strong box.

"The Maid Alisande has revealed herself," Clarence reported. "She is talking to your twin brother."

Tom crossed to the slot. "He's *not* my brother, I tell you. He's a humanoid — a robot. I've *programmed* him to joust for me."

"If thou say so," Clarence said politely. "But Maid Alisande is giving the — er, robot — quite a program herself."

Tom took a small radio receiver from his pocket and extended the antennae.

"What next!" marveled Clarence.

"Sssh."

Sandy's voice was the first to be heard. "Oh, Thomas, I wouldn't dare speak this way if I thought I'd ever be facing you again. But since you're going to be killed anyway, I see no harm in revealing my strange feelings for you."

"Listen to that, Clarence!" Tom exclaimed. "I think she likes me."

"I think she likes your brother."

"Sssh! Listen."

"Thomas," Sandy murmured, "I really don't know who or what you are, but these pangs I feel must be love. I haven't felt like this since my favorite cow, Gwendolyn, was taken off to market and I knew I'd never see her again."

Tom frowned down at Sandy. No girl had ever told him that he meant as much to her as a *cow*. "Would you say that's love, Clarence?"

But Clarence was too worried about their safety to get really lost in romance. "We have no time for this. I dare not think what form Sir Mordred's wrath might take if his servants discovered us."

Tom might have turned back to Sir Mordred's strong box if Hermes hadn't at this moment swooped Sandy up and pressed his visor closely to her lips. "All right, Hermes! That's enough. Put her down. Get on with the joust. *Hermes! Put that girl down. That's an order!*"

Slowly, Hermes lowered Sandy to the ground. "You feel soft," he said.

"*Soft*? Thomas, thou nearly brokest my neck! Is that all you have to say?"

"Later," replied Hermes.

Tom gasped. "He's programmed to react to sights and sounds, but *this*! It's sheer insubordination!" He spoke again into the transmitter. "Hermes, there's not going to be any later. Remember, I can turn you off as fast as she can turn you on."

Clarence nudged Tom. "Please. Get whatever you seek and let us vacate these chambers."

"Okay. You keep watching down there."

"Trumpeters are now calling the charge," Clarence reported.

In the jousting lane Sir Mordred took a firm grip on his lance. Hermes, watching closely, did the same thing. King Arthur arose, holding a scarf high. As the last note from the trumpets sounded, he dropped the fluttering signal to the ground. Sir Mordred's steed lurched forward.

Hermes' mount, not used to high falutin' Court games, looked calmly ahead. "Giddap!" Hermes urged. Off the pair started, in a clop-clopping sort of way.

Sir Mordred's experience showed. With the first blow of his lance, Hermes' arm went flying off. In spite of this awful injury, Hermes went galloping onward, lance still leveled.

"What magnificent courage and horsemanship!" King Arthur gasped.

"Should someone not notify yon Thomas that his arm is missing?" asked Sir Gawain.

"Against the rules," the King replied sadly. "I made them myself."

Tom gazed through the binoculars. "That should be satisfaction enough for Mordred. Look what he did!"

"I fear not," Clarence shook his head. "This joust is to the death."

Tom radioed Hermes. "Sorry. Turn around, Hermes. It's the rules. You keep going until — " he hesitated. "Until you can't."

Hermes gallantly turned his mount and jogged past his own arm lying on the ground. He never so much as glanced at it.

"I've never seen such raw courage, Merlin," King Arthur said, pausing before signaling a second charge.

"Creatures of the lower orders can lose an appendage and still survive, Your Highness," replied the highly educated Merlin.

"I have little enthusiasm for this contest," said the King. "Pitting a professional like Mordred against a poor dumb animal."

Sandy buried her face in Father's feathers as the King dropped the scarf again. "Oh, Father, I can't look. I *do* love him!"

It was a good thing for Maid Alisande that she had Father along with her. She might not have been able to stand the dreadful result of the second charge. This time Sir Mordred, deciding on a sudden-death match, leveled his lance even with his opponent's head.

Even such experienced joust-goers as lived in Camelot could scarcely bear the result of this action. The sight was too much. Indeed, a few quietly slipped through the bleachers to the ground below, unable to look any longer at the headless rider on the white horse.

"How's Hermes doing?" Tom asked Clarence.

Clarence lowered the binoculars. "Not well," he replied. "He seems to have lost his head."

"Don't worry about Hermes, Clarence. He's cool."

"Cool? He's cold!" Clarence exclaimed. He handed over the binoculars. "Take a look."

Tom looked. "Oh! You meant he *lost his head*." He radioed, "Sorry, Hermes. But it's to save England."

Hermes, already programmed to joust until he could joust no more, swung his mount for a third tilt at Sir Mordred. This time Sir Mordred was determined to put an end to the jousting match. With this in mind he skewered Hermes right off his horse and directly in front of His Highness.

King Arthur lifted his hand to his eyes. "At least It is out of Its misery."

Sir Gawain fought back a tear. "Perhaps even now the poor creature's spirit flies back to that 'Cape' he spoke of so longingly. *Look*!"

King Arthur looked. Sparks and smoke curls plumed up from the downed Hermes' wounds. Wires, wheels, and assorted computer parts spun through the air. Sandy, caring nothing of her own safety, rushed on the scene ready to throw herself and Father on her newly discovered great love. But even she dodged back as a center spring *boinged* fearfully from Hermes' chest.

"Hurry!" Clarence begged, turning away from the carnage below.

"How's Hermes?" Tom asked, sorting through papers in the strong box.

"Done for."

"I'm sorry I spoke to him so sharply. But maybe I can put him back together again."

"Not all the King's horses nor all the King's men are going to do that," Clarence said sadly.

Tom jumped up. "This is it! I've found the evidence!" He waved a handful of parchment scrolls — land deeds — over his head.

"Then let us depart, now!"

They hurried from the room. "Wait 'til King Arthur gets a load of *this*!" Tom exclaimed.

King Arthur, members of his Court, and Sandy were still viewing the sad remains in the jousting lane. "A pity," said the King. "I was becoming rather attached to It — whatever It was."

"No longer will it be a source of torment," said Sir Mordred as he bowed from his seat on his charger. "I have sent the creature from our midst for all time."

Sandy, in a state of shock, couldn't even

run from the dread Mordred. But Merlin kept his wits together as he viewed the hardware. "With your permission, Sire, I'll keep the remains for my laboratory. I might gain insight into its origin and feeding habits."

"As you wish." King Arthur replied. "But tidy up thoroughly."

Merlin's voice brought Sandy back to her other sad problem. "Merlin, Sire, I wonder if I might beg of you to change my father back into his old self?"

Merlin flashed a quick look at Mordred. He raised his hand. "Later, my child. More important matters demand my attention at the moment."

"You and the gander can wait in my quarters," said Mordred. "Guards, escort the maid!"

A voice rang out. *"All right! As you were!"*

And into the very middle of Camelot's highest society strode Tom Trimble, computer engineer of Kennedy Space Center, Cape Canaveral, Florida, U.S.A.

If his duplicate face of the late Hermes was not enough to cause ladies to faint and knights to stagger backwards, his costume did it. Sports coats and slacks were far from being the fashion in Camelot.

"Okay," he cried out, "everybody stay right

there. And you, Merlin, keep your mitts off Hermes."

"Someone, fetch my physician," murmured a pale King Arthur.

"One moment, Your Majesty," said Tom. "First I'd like to present some documentary proof that Mordred here is preparing for a Camelot takeover. Land. Arms. Men. The works."

Weakly, the King began to examine the parchment scrolls. He seemed to get his strength back rapidly as he read. "How do you come into such large holdings, Knight?" he asked coldly. "I see by these you've also been acting as your own tax collector. To what end? Well?"

While Mordred cast about for a really first-class answer, Tom filled the gap.

"The end is to hire mercenaries to take Camelot by force. And as Camelot goes, so goes England!"

King Arthur turned a royal purple. *"Seize that Knight,"* he roared.

But Mordred was not standing still for *that*. He reared his black charger in dramatic fashion. "Death to Arthur!" he yelled.

All was confusion — and before it was sorted out, the Black Knight made good his escape!

8

Almost from that moment, there was nothing too good for Tom Trimble as far as King Arthur was concerned. At Tom's request, all Camelot assisted in moving *Stardust One* from its original landing place to the castle courtyard.

Even Merlin gave his full cooperation by chaining off the gleaming white spaceship and hanging out a sign:

> U.S. GOVERNMENT PROPERTY
> KEEP OFF — THIS MEANS YOU
> *Merlin*

In the Round Table room of the castle, King Arthur, Sir Gawain, and Sandy were in attendance upon Dr. Tom. Acting as head surgeon, with Sandy as scrub nurse, he was performing delicate surgery upon Hermes. Father padded and waddled around this royal operating theater and respectfully refrained from honking.

"Drill," Surgeon Tom demanded, holding out his hand.

Sandy slapped over a monkey wrench. Luckily, she didn't throw it into the machinery, but Tom gave her a dirty look all the same. He reached for a power drill.

Smoke curled up from Hermes' wounds as the drill reached the high-pitched whine of a dentist's instrument. King Arthur, Sir Gawain, and Sandy all winced, and showed signs of suffering — far more acutely than the patient.

"There's something unholy about this," said His Majesty, looking pale. "Maybe it's best that he die in peace."

But Tom answered most cheerfully, "It's really not as bad as I thought. I can bypass his metabolic synthesizer and still keep his voice command analyzer functioning."

"Maybe you could do something about Father, too, when you're through," Sandy said hopefully.

"Sandy, I tell you I saw your father alive in the castle. I talked with him. He was *not* a gander."

"Are you certain?" Sandy asked, frowning.

"Certain."

Unnoticed, Merlin came skulking through the door just as Sir Gawain said, "I've been meaning to tell you, Thomas. Your after-dinner entertainment is far more amusing than watching Merlin turn a mouse into a glass of wine. I'm getting awfully tired of that."

"Upstart!" Merlin muttered.

"Sir Gawain," His Highness said, "I wish you'd concern yourself more about an attack by Mordred and his forces, and less about pleasure." Then he turned to Tom. "And I'd like to thank you, Thomas, for revealing Mordred's treachery. Is there not some way we can repay you?"

"Well," Tom began, while fusing another wire of Hermes' circulatory system, "now that you mention it, King. . . I did notice a couple of vacant seats here at the Round Table. I'd consider it a real privilege to become a member."

King Arthur looked troubled. "I'm afraid it's not that simple. We have many applicants, naturally. We can't take in every Tom, Dick, and Harris that applies. There are certain requirements. You see, Tom, you haven't slain a dragon . . . or rescued a maiden or done anything that demonstrates courage."

"The King is right, Thomas," Sandy piped up.

Tom looked at her briefly. "Mmm. Well, thanks anyway, King. I just thought it might be something to tell the grandchildren. 'Sir Tom Trimble — Knight of the Round Table.' Has a kind of ring to it."

"Not like Sir Galahad or Sir Lancelot," Sandy promptly said. "Now *those* are names."

King Arthur looked down at Hermes. "He seems to be holding up well. I believe I must be off, though, and check the castle defenses. I'm worried about Mordred."

Followed by Sir Gawain, he departed, failing to notice Merlin in the shadows.

Tom worked on with Hermes a little longer. "There! That's about all I can do until I get into his pneumatically actuated finger reflexes." He gave Hermes a friendly pat. "Hang in there, Hermes. We'll have you up and about in no time."

"Okay," Hermes whispered.

"No hard feelings about the joust, are there?"

Hermes made no reply and Sandy touched him tenderly. "You're so brave," she murmured.

Her hero gave a little contented moan and Tom quietly pressed an *off* switch. Right away Hermes went limp. His eyes closed and his repaired head rolled to one side.

"Don't worry," said Tom. "He's resting comfortably."

From his corner, Merlin hadn't missed Tom's switch-pressing. He stored this information away for future use and kept on eavesdropping.

"How'd you like a personally conducted tour of *Stardust One*?" Tom asked.

"Oh, I think not."

"I've probably got some L.P.s in there you probably haven't heard. Some country and Dixieland."

"Thanks anyway — but no," Sandy said coolly.

Tom looked puzzled. "Why the hot and cold bit? You said before the joust that you kind of dug me."

Sandy blushed. "I made an awful fool of myself. I didn't know who or *what* I was talking to. I bared my heart to — to your brother here. And it turns out he's full of wheels and junk. I'm not saying he isn't *nice*, but . . . I really shouldn't get involved with that sort of thing."

"Look, Miss Maid Alisande, I'm just as human as you are. I had a mother and a father. He's an optometrist in Poughkeepsie. I squeaked through Grover Cleveland High, but I got a Master's at Valley U. and lettered in the high hurdles. I took Mona Shanks to the senior prom — batted 'O' for 'O.' What more can I say? I'm just an average American boy. Can't you understand that?"

"No. Well, I must be running along. I still haven't been able to get any cooperation from Merlin." She turned away and picked up Father.

That night Tom, with King Arthur and Sir Gawain, made a tour of Camelot's defenses. Merlin again tagged along. Arrows were stockpiled. Crossbows were being tested. And bonfires were being lighted to heat pots of boiling oil for pouring down on the enemy.

"Keep a sharp eye," King Arthur warned a lieutenant.

"Fear not, Sire," the young officer said bravely. "We shall defend our castle whatever the cost may be. We shall fight on the landings, we shall fight in the courtyards, we shall fight in the halls. We shall never surrender." He thoughtfully added, "And we would fight on the beachheads, too, if we only had beachheads."

"Well, I'll be darned," Tom muttered. "Somewhere, sometime I heard a similar speech. But when? Where?"

But King Arthur only nodded. "Well said, Winston," he said, and the inspection tour went on. Tom continued to look puzzled.

Then Sir Gawain changed the subject and

Tom thought no more of Winston the Speechmaker. "In all probability they'll come from the north," Sir Gawain said.

"They'll come from the south," King Arthur snapped.

"That's what I meant, Sire. South. Then I fear it will mean a long siege."

King Arthur stopped in his tracks. "Gawain, you fool! It won't be a siege. Mordred will make a direct assault on the battlements with battering rams and superior forces."

Sir Gawain nodded quickly. "I was going to add there is that distinct possibility."

For the first time Tom entered the conversation. "They'll have to cross the moat first, and I think I have the answer to that problem."

"You do? You think the haycart not enough of a barrier?"

Tom took out his laser-beam pistol. He aimed and fired at the sturdy cart below. Before the startled eyes of all, especially Merlin's, who'd been tagging along, the haycart went up in smoke.

"What sorcery hast thou now, American!" King Arthur exclaimed.

"It's called a laser gun. Hermes was going to use it for excavation on other planets — to gather rock and soil samples."

"May I examine it?"

Tom hesitated. "Okay, but don't point it at anything you want to keep."

King Arthur thought that over. "A cart is a cart. But let me see its effect, if any, against the solid stones of Camelot."

Taking aim, His Majesty blasted an unused castle turret. In a huge flash of light, heavy stones and mortar fell heavily into the courtyard below. Castle personnel dashed for safety.

"Well — what do you think?" Tom grinned, taking back the gun.

"I, for one," began Sir Gawain, "have always held you in highest regard. And I hope we'll always be friends." He bowed. "Respectfully, your obedient servant."

"Gawain, *will* you cease thy fawning prattle. That is a very dangerous weapon. It must not fall into the wrong hands."

"Don't worry, King," said Tom. "I keep it handy at all times."

Merlin's dark eyes narrowed. "We'll see about that," he muttered. He turned the other way. "The thing to do next is get Oaf in on this."

Oaf! It was a name to make prisoners tremble — as Mr. Watkins could swear to. But Merlin and Mordred had often found Oaf a useful brute to have around when there was dirty work to be done.

Merlin made his way to the dungeon regions and found Oaf on the job of making prisoners confess crimes that never had happened. "Oaf," he began, "I'm taking you off torture duty and putting you on a new assignment. I think you're going to love it."

As quickly as possible he outlined his plan to the slow-witted Oaf. "First, it's going to be impossible for Mordred to take Camelot with Thomas the American about. But I have a good idea how to get rid of him."

Oaf crushed his huge hands together. "Oaf kill!" he grinned.

"Not just yet, Oaf. The King would order an investigation and we don't want that, do we?"

Oaf shook his head.

"But there's more than one way to skin a cat," Merlin said.

A smile once again brightened Oaf's face. "Whose cat?" he asked eagerly.

"Now, Oaf! You must wait. Right now I want you to find that crazy girl who seeks her father. Tell her that Merlin the Magician will see her *now* — in the *lower* chamber. Got that?"

Oaf repeated the instructions.

"Good. For that you shall have your favorite — raw chicken." He tossed Oaf a package. "After you get her here, take her through the secret passage to the woods beyond. And *keep* her there. I'll take care of the American.

"Now *do* you understand your job?" Merlin asked. "Bring her to me, then await further instructions."

Between crunches of a drumstick, Oaf nodded.

Merlin watched him thumping along the gloomy corridor. He shook his head. "Hard to get good help these days. Hope he doesn't blow it. Now for the next step — that laser gun."

9

Camelot by moonlight was very pretty, and *Stardust One* had never rested in a more beautiful setting than the castle courtyard.

Tom Trimble, escorted by a servant, walked over to the gleaming white spacecraft. He looked around, puzzled. "Where is she? I don't see her."

"I know not, Sire. I was only informed the Maid Alisande wished to meet you here. She wanted to see some of your . . . L.P.'s."

"Oh. That's right. I mentioned that to her."

The servant bowed and moved off. Tom glanced at his wristwatch. "Wonder what's keeping her?" he muttered. "Oh, well — I'll wait."

Upstairs in the castle, Merlin was making

good use of Tom's absence from his room. Frantically he searched Tom's few belongings. "Not here. Not here," he muttered. "Where *does* he keep it?" He reached beneath Tom's pillow and an evil grin creased his face. "Ah ha!" Triumphantly, he pulled forth the precious laser gun!

In the dungeon corridors, Sandy, with Father, followed Oaf. "Now you be nice to the Magician," Sandy warned. "Don't go pecking his finger. Remember, he's here to help you."

They turned a corner, and in the dim light of a smoky torch Sandy saw an old hag seated at a desk by a doorway. "Merlin is expecting us," she said politely.

"Please be seated," the hag crackled.

They had not long to wait. Through a concealed door in the room beyond, Merlin, panting and puffing, returned from his successful raid of Tom's quarters. Breathless, he pulled a cord hanging along the wall. A tiny bell rang on the hag's desk. "The Magician will see you now," she announced.

Merlin's office seemed to suit his personality. Although dimly lighted, a small fire took the chill off the room. Shelves were lined by stuffed animals and owls, small apothecary jars, and on the walls were framed parchments listing Merlin's many awards in the All Magicians Association.

Now he smiled at her disarmingly, and

97

Sandy was sure Father would walk out of the office, once more a freeman.

"Well, now — what seems to be the trouble?" Merlin asked.

"Oh, I'm fine, Sire. It's Father here. You see — Ooof!"

That was as far as her explanation went. Oaf popped a heavy sack over her head.

"Quickly," she heard Merlin say.

Oaf dragged her to the exact center of the stone floor. Then, lifting a huge rock slab cleverly concealing a secret passage beneath the moat and through the woods beyond, he began to drag his struggling captive from view.

"Wait!" cried Merlin. "Get rid of that goose!

"No! Not that way!" Merlin ordered. "There'll be feathers all over the place. Here! Push it out through the slot!"

Father squawked and fluttered but soon found himself quite comfortably floating in the moat outside the castle walls.

In the castle's Great Hall, Clarence watched nervously as Tom, with Hermes' help, worked on a homemade parchment and metal model of *Stardust One*.

"Is it going to make that big noise again?" he asked.

Tom mounted the model on a tilted sword

blade he was using as a launch ramp. "I hope not. I had the cotton packed too tightly last time. That's why it exploded."

"You see, Clarence," Hermes explained, "Tom's trying to get *thrust* to propel the craft into the air. Can't you see that?" He turned to Tom. "Where's Sandy?"

"Forget Sandy," Tom replied. "I cooled my heels long enough waiting outdoors for her and she never showed up. She and I are through. And you put her out of your mind, too, Hermes."

Hermes sighed. "That's not easy."

At that moment the charge in the propulsion system of the little craft ignited. Zigzagging crazily like a balloon driven by expelled air, it swooped toward the entrance just in time to catch Sir Gawain in the chest. Naturally, Sir Gawain defended himself and nailed it with the tip of his sword. "Oh, *dear*!" he cried. "Your model! I'm *so* sorry."

King Arthur looked down at the demolished model. "I hope you're as handy with that sword when Mordred attacks."

Honk! Father's familiar one-word vocabulary sounded and resounded throughout the Great Hall. "Sandy!" Tom spun around in time to see Winston marching toward the kitchen, Father under his arm. "Hey! What have you got there?" he asked.

Winston looked puzzled. "A goose, as anyone can plainly see."

"It's a gander and no one can plainly see," Tom replied. "Where did you find him?"

"In the moat. He paddled right up to me. He'll make a fine supper."

Tom took Father into his own arms. "What about the girl? Where was she?"

Winston's eyes widened. "There was no girl about. Just 'im. But we did hear a woman's screams from yon woods. I paid no mind, thinking it just one of the village lasses carrying on. In fact, I saw her and Oaf going toward Merlin's. That was earlier, though."

It was Tom's turn to stare. "I've been *duped*!" he cried.

He dashed from the Hall, King Arthur and the others following close at his heels as Tom sped to his room and lifted the bed-pillow. "It's gone! The laser gun is gone!"

"Who would take it?" King Arthur frowned.

"Merlin! He tricked me out of here by a message that Sandy was waiting for me by *Stardust*."

King Arthur was grim-faced. "Mordred. Now Merlin!"

"Exactly. They're in cahoots. They're partners!" He turned to Winston. "Where do you think they would take her?"

"To Mordred's camp, most likely."

"You're not thinking of going after the wench!" King Arthur exclaimed.

"Don't be rash," added Sir Gawain. "There's a difference between knight errantry and foolishness. Besides, why not go after the gun — not the girl?"

Tom brushed this aside. "The poor kid needs help. And *I'll* need your armor, King."

"Tom — you keep forgetting you're still a prisoner here, and I do not go about lending my personal armor to prisoners. The answer is — *no*."

"Then Mordred will reduce Camelot to dust."

King Arthur hesitated. "Well — maybe my work-a-day armor."

"No. I must have your heaviest, best Sunday-go-to-meetin' armor. And the shiniest you've got."

There was a short silence. King and prisoner stared at each other. King Arthur was the first to look away. "Fetch it, Clarence," he said briefly.

In the forest, Merlin consulted with Mordred. "If he takes the bait," Mordred said, "we attack at dawn." He hefted the laser gun. "But not before I dispatch the American with his own weapon."

Merlin grinned. "Even the gates of Camelot cannot withstand such power. This thing will put battering rams and crossbows completely out of date. See for yourself, Mordred. Throw the force against yon ancient oak."

Mordred aimed, fired — and the oak tree, a good fifty yards away, burst into flames and thundered to the forest floor.

Merlin chuckled. "The American will disappear in a cloud of smoke."

Sandy jumped up from her position at the base of a nearby tree. "You are wicked, wicked men," she cried. "*Both* of you."

"Silence, Maid!" Mordred roared. "Or I shall leave you to Oaf's mercy here and now."

Sandy dropped to the ground weeping. And Mordred turned his attention to starting his forces on to Camelot.

In the castle courtyard, King Arthur, together with Camelot's finest knights, clustered around the spacecraft. They all took a step backwards as a siren sounded and a panel lowered to form a ramp to the ground.

Down it rode Tom at the wheel of a Moon Rover. He came to a stop before the King and held up an armored arm. "The suit's a little long in the sleeves, but the chest plate couldn't be better. Clarence shined it up to perfection."

His Majesty shook his head. "I don't understand all this over a mere snip of a girl!"

"Lower the drawbridge, please," Tom grinned.

"*I* say when the bridge is lowered, Prisoner," the King reminded Tom.

"Sorry. But we've got to hurry. Hold the fort 'til I get back."

Off he went, bouncing over the drawbridge.

"Alas! He's never coming back," the King sighed. "Close the drawbridge!"

"We'll miss his lies," Sir Gawain said sadly.

King Arthur frowned. "Let's ask his brother about them. Come."

Hermes was no help in proving Tom's honesty. He shook his head at all questions. "No. I never heard about the Nina, Pinta, and the Santa Maria, or any of that other stuff."

"I was afraid of that," King Arthur sighed gloomily. "Now how can we depend on such as Thomas? He's given no thought to the lost laser gun. Probably he has his mind on making up more ridiculous stories to tell that ridiculous girl. What becomes of Camelot if Mordred gets that dread weapon in his hands?"

The sound of knocking knees was the only answer that reached his ears.

★ ★ ★

In Sir Mordred's camp a sentry raced past horses and grouping soldiers. "Sir Mordred," he panted, "something approacheth by the stream."

"Something?"

"Sire, it has two eyes that light up the night and it makes strange breathing noises."

Mordred grabbed the laser gun. "Lead me to it!" he demanded.

Merlin was little help. Although he followed Mordred along with a trusted group of bowmen, he could offer no useful information. "It is not a dragon for it has no tail. Yet its eyes can blind one. And its breath seems not to issue forth from the standard position of the nose."

Tom pulled the Moon Rover to a stop and awkwardly clanked out of it. There was no doubt — the sleeves and legs of his outfit needed taking in. But their lack of fit was more than made up for by the glorious golden armor. "T'is King Arthur himself," cried out the bowmen.

Tom lifted his visor. "No, it's not King Arthur. It's me — Tom Trimble. I've come for the Maid Alisande."

Sandy rushed forward. "Oh, Tom! You shouldn't have come. They plan to kill you!"

"And with *your* choice of weapons," Mordred grinned. He aimed the laser gun.

"Get behind me, Sandy," Tom ordered.

"That will serve little purpose," Merlin sneered helpfully. "We've seen the awesome power of the magic candle. It will annihilate you both in a flash." He bowed to Mordred. "Pray do the honors, Mordred."

"Any parting words, American?" Mordred asked.

"Yeah. I'd like to talk with Sandy a second."

"Be brief."

"Sandy," Tom whispered, "if we don't pull this off, I want you to know I really groove on you."

"Groove?" Sandy stared.

"I mean — I'd really like to take the five-fifteen home every night and there'd you'd be — waiting to split a pizza with me. And maybe we could — well, what do you say, Sandy?"

"Any news of Father?" Sandy asked anxiously.

"*Sandy!* I just told you I love you and that's all you have to say?"

Sandy looked sad. "I'm not going through that sort of thing *twice*. I'd pledge my troth to you and then find you're stuffed with feathers or old corn husks. Really — that's no better than wheels and wires, is it?"

Tom sighed. But Sandy had more to say.

"On the other hand, if it's a choice between you and Oaf — well, I'd choose you."

Tom glanced over at the hideous Oaf. "Thank you, Sandy. I'll always remember that — that you have *great* judgment. How'd you ever make up your mind?"

"Enough!" Sir Mordred bellowed.

"Fire at will," Tom said proudly, stepping in front of Sandy.

There was a blinding flash of light. Tom grunted slightly, then watched the shot, that had bounced off his gleaming gold chest, angle off into the trees of Sir Mordred's camp. A second shot did spectacular damage to the enemy.

"Mordred! Cease!" cried Merlin. "You'll destroy your entire force!"

Mordred stared at his combat organization and then at the gun. "He's bewitched it!" he cried, and fired one last shot.

Fortunately, for all concerned, a falling tree buried the laser gun, and Tom cried, "Let's go!" He rushed Sandy into the Moon Rover.

"Stop them!" Mordred bellowed.

Almost instantly a swarm of arrows and spears zinged after the Moon Rover. "Duck!" Tom cried out, pushing Sandy forward.

It was no use. Mordred's weapon penetrated the Moon Rover's wire-mesh wheels.

Progress was impossible. Sandy huddled close to Tom.

"Seize them. Hold them under guard. I'll settle with them later," cried Mordred.

Fearfully, Sandy peeked over Tom's elbow. "Here comes that Oaf," she groaned. "And guards! Oh, Thomas! We are indeed done for."

Tom added a groan of his own as five stalwart guards surrounded the moon buggy. "If I'd had radial steel-belted tires, the course of history could have been changed," he said sadly.

"On to Camelot!" roared Mordred.

Cheers went up from the soldiers. In a few minutes Tom and Sandy were left with guards — all alone in the forest.

10

The Battle of Camelot would long be remembered.

True, there were the same old pots of boiling oil ready to be poured from the ramparts. And there were the same expert crossbowmen ready to die for King and Camelot. All Camelot could see that King Arthur and his forces were doing their best.

But Mordred's men had already infiltrated the castle — thanks to Merlin's leaving the stone slab trapdoor open for one and all.

Mordred, at the secret opening, heard the clang of a sword.

"Quiet, you clod!" he rasped out. "Surprise is our greatest weapon. If we catch them unaware, Camelot will be mine in an hour."

"And with it, all England," Merlin added gleefully.

From their lonely post in the forest Sandy watched for signs of fire in the sky over the castle. So far, only the moon and stars lighted the heavens.

Tom wasn't as interested in sky-watching as Oaf-watching. And it struck him that Sandy was in greater danger in the moon buggy than was King Arthur in his castle. Unlike the camp guards who were bored, now they were no longer in the thick of battle, Oaf kept alert — and close.

Memories of the Cape in happier days flitted through Tom's head. Plain as day he could see the design plans of the Moon Rover stretched out on his drawing board. He frowned. "What is there about the moon buggy that keeps bugging me?" he muttered.

Suddenly he had it! The jet seat! And with a happy whistle to show just how relaxed he was, he slid his hands around the seat edge searching for the blast-off release.

"What are you doing?" Sandy asked loudly.

"Nothing," Tom replied merrily, while wishing he could put adhesive tape over her pretty mouth.

"How can you say 'nothing' when I can

plainly see you're tinkering with this seat?"

Oaf stepped closer. Quickly, Tom tossed out a foil-wrapped K-ration; it landed at Oaf's large feet. As Merlin's favorite brute bent to pick it up, Tom reached for the soil-sampler arm. Deftly he guided it above Oaf's neck. The steam-shovel type prongs grabbed out. Thump! Oaf's head bounced hard against the ground.

"Quick, Sandy! Sit on my lap," Tom ordered.

"Thomas! I'll do no such thing!"

There was nothing to do but pull the reluctant Maid Alisande over on his lap. Oaf was losing no time in getting out of the soil sampler's clutches. But his savage roar of anger was lost in a bigger roar as Tom gave the jet seat full throttle.

Guards and Oaf stared up bewildered as their prisoners shot straight upward and twin red jets plumed out behind.

Sandy looked down fearfully. "Maybe you'd better put your arms around me — tight. It's safer," Tom yelled in her ear.

Sandy needed no second invitation. She nearly choked him. "Are you taking me to your nest?" she asked at the top of her voice.

"Camelot," Tom yelled back. "I just hope it still has the same landlord as when we left."

The battle was going poorly for King Arthur's defenders, owing to Mordred's excellent planning of attack from the inside as well as the outside.

But it was an enemy soldier who made the first fatal mistake — he looked up at a moving light in the sky. *Boingg!* Down he went as Winston took quick advantage of his inattention.

Up on the battlements, another Mordred team member also looked up for a quick glimpse of this strange sight. Sir Gawain, gentle as he was square, gave the intruder a gentle push. The clank of metal on stone signaled his successful contribution as a fighting man. Then he, too, saw the whizzing light in the sky.

Soon, swords on both sides hung idle as all stood spellbound, eyes riveted on the fast descending dive-bomber.

Pausing only long enough to drop off Sandy with the Ladies of the Court, Tom whizzed upward. Merlin, in his long, black flowing robes, was easy to spot among the military personnel. Lowering the soil-sampler arm, Tom neatly removed the Magician from action. And Mordred watched awestruck as his dearest friend sailed high over the castle wall. Then a giant splashing sound made it clear to all ears that Merlin the Magician had become Merlin of the Moat.

Back Tom boomed — this time he dropped a Mordred man who was leading a column of fighting men in a charge up a staircase. It was the domino effect at its best! The Mordred soldier toppled onto the man behind him, and one after another the column of armored men clanked in a heap of metal at the bottom of the stairs.

Next, Tom directed a jet blast to the pants-seats of an entire company. Smoking-hot, the outfit, to a man, hit the moat as fast as possible.

"Singlehandedly he turns the tide of battle!" cried King Arthur. And on Tom's next swoop, he gave the daring pilot a thumbs-up salute. "Good show, American!" he shouted.

"Never have so many owed so much to one man," Winston gasped.

Sir Gawain smiled gently. "What a nice thought."

But in the sky, Tom caught an ominous sound. "Either I got an arrow in the jet pack or I'm out of gas! My goose is going to be cooked!"

It was that word "goose" that snapped him back to a fighting mood. "After all, I saved Father from cooking. I sure can't give up my own goose," he muttered.

Then the only logical solution hit him.

"Hermes!" he called into the radio. "Fire engine one . . . engine two."

Results were even better than he'd expected. Just the roar of the powerful engines sent Mordred's forces into panic. Cries filled the air. "Run for your lives!" "The great bird is alive."

Mordred was hard put to rally his men. "Do not fear the contraption. It has no power. *Slay the American!*"

Tom gave all his attention to his radio. "Hermes, right vernier thrust, ten degrees. Engage right vernier thruster."

To his satisfaction he saw a jet blast send several of Mordred's men galley-west. Then, purposefully, he glided down to the ground directly in line with *Stardust One*'s nose and those of Mordred's forces still standing on their feet.

"Destroy the American!" Mordred screamed. "Destroy!"

Again Tom spoke calmly into the radio. "Engage magnetic field, engine one."

Hermes flipped a lever. A strange whining sound pierced the air. One intake wing swung open. Mordred's armored forces were caught like dust in the path of a vacuum cleaner. Men, swords, shields, axes, spears — all were packed sardine-style against the side of *Stardust One*.

"Engage magnetic field . . . engine two."

More enemy personnel were immediately added to the first heap of Mordred's failing forces. And in all the clanks of piling-up armor and yells of piling-up soldiers, Merlin arrived unnoticed from his dip in the moat.

Looking like a trailing bundle of wet wash, he slipped up close to *Stardust One* and — Hermes. His scientific mind told him that unless he could end the robot's power, he and Mordred faced a very dim future.

If Hermes hadn't been concentrating on Tom's radio instructions, he certainly would have heard Merlin's squishy footsteps behind him. But at the very moment Merlin bent toward him, Tom's voice flooded the cabin with the opening bars of the National Anthem. *"Oh-o say can you see — "*

Up went Hermes' rocklike fist in a snappy salute. But in between his fist and his forehead was Merlin's entire damp dome. Down went the Magician. Calmly, Hermes reclosed the cabin door and turned back to the controls.

Outside, Sir Mordred, sword drawn, advanced. With a mighty slash aimed over the head of the National Anthem vocalist, he brought the blade downward. Had it not been for *Stardust*'s sudden magnetic pull, Tom Trimble would never have had a chance to

sing *"through bombs burst in air . . ."* But
Mordred suddenly joined the ranks of en-
listed men sprawled in a heap at the base of
the spaceship.

In the cabin, Merlin staggered to his feet.
Almost blindly he pressed a button. Down
went the steps from the nose of *Stardust One*.
And up went Mordred's remaining forces.

Tom reacted in horror. At the very moment
of triumph the battle was turning!

"Hermes!" he yelled. "The ramp! Quick!"

Instantly the enemy, to the last man, came
sliding back at top speed as the steps beneath
them turned into a chute.

It was "all clear" for the loyal royal side,
and up came King Arthur and all the King's
men. Tom waved his hand toward the vanquished enemy. "Take 'em downtown and
book 'em!" He grinned.

"Much as we'd like you and Hermes to stay
on forever in Camelot, we know that loyalty
to your own country comes first," King Arthur said sadly. "But we do have a small surprise for you, Thomas. Come."

His Majesty, followed by the Court, led
Tom through the Great Hall and on to the
Round Table. Tom immediately recognized
the elderly man bending over the table and
blowing away a few curls of wood — Sandy's

father! No wonder she had been so happy all morning!

"Please look at our Chief Woodcarver's work, Thomas," said the King.

Tom swallowed hard. There was the name *Tom Trimble* and below it a coat-of-arms. Mr. Watkins had carved a very neat American flag beside the *Stardust One*. "Gee!" he gulped. "I don't know what to say. That's really distinguished company." He read aloud, "Sir Galahad, Sir Lancelot, King Arthur."

"Sir Gawain," said Sir Gawain.

Tom nodded. "They're never gonna believe this at the Cape."

King Arthur smiled. "I will retire this chair, Thomas."

Tom gasped. "Like retiring a baseball player's number!"

"I suppose so," His Majesty said politely. "But to go on — If ever thou returneth, your place at the Round Table will be here, waiting."

"They're *never* going to believe this at the Cape," Tom repeated. Then suddenly he picked up his canvas flight bag and dug out a camera. "Yes, they *will* believe it! King Arthur — now you stand right there. Sandy, get in on the other side. Mr. Watkins — you, too. Move in close."

"This is very unusual," His Majesty said.

Finally, Tom had everybody together. "Now, everybody, say 'cheese.'" The flash went off and Sir Gawain's hand went to his sword. In the nick of time, Tom rescued the processed film that popped out.

Except for Sandy, who had a very silly look as she'd said 'cheese,' the picture was excellent.

The group was still marveling over the picture when Merlin, in light chains, went by with guards at either side. It was plain that the Magician wanted to see why the American and Sandy were smiling so happily even though something mysterious had just flashed in their faces. But the guards prodded him forward.

Tom looked at the developed film, then snapped a second picture. "Show that to Merlin when he gets out on good behavior," he said proudly. "He'll eat his heart out."

"Oh, quite right," His Majesty agreed.

Tom held out his hand. "Well, King, I guess this is it. I'm off. Hermes will be wondering whatever happened to me. Now take care of yourself!"

Sir Gawain could not help but notice that Thomas turned to make a special good-bye to the Maid Alisande. He would have edged closer had not King Arthur led him away.

Tom looked into Sandy's lovely eyes.

"I'd — I'd like to take you with me, Sandy. There are so many things I want to show you — my old MG, my ten speed, Space Mountain, Fisherman's Wharf."

"That would be very nice." Sandy nodded.

"But I don't know if you'd survive the trip. You could age a thousand years before we even reentered."

It seemed only polite to agree with the Hero of the Battle of Camelot, even if she didn't understand a word he was saying. She nodded again. "And thanks again for getting Merlin to change Father back into Father."

Tom's eyes rolled skyward. "Think nothing of it," he replied grandly, just as if he'd had nothing to do with the recent discovery of the prisoner, Watkins.

Sandy held out a note. "Will you give this to Hermes, please?"

Together they walked out to the courtyard.

This time at the launching of *Stardust One* there were no cameras, no Dr. Zimmerman, and no nationwide TV hookup. But in their place stood — the King!

His Majesty stood at a distance from Camelot's tilted drawbridge which was serving as a launch-pad. He stood, finger just over an electric switch. ". . . six . . . five . . . four . . . three . . . two . . . ignition." He pressed the button. "We have lift-off!"

Clouds of smoke set the Court to coughing, but slowly, slowly *Stardust* rose, then disappeared into the blue.

High in their cabin in the sky, Tom handed Sandy's note to Hermes. Lips moving, Hermes read it. Tom turned the speaker volume up. *"Dear Hermes, I think you are sweet, and I will always remember you fondly. But there can never be anything between us. I have given the matter much thought, and I like Tom best. It was not an easy decision. . . ."*

Stardust One gained speed in space. "I hope we're winding the clock the right way," said Tom.

"Already it's the year 680."

"Good man, Hermes."

A loud *honk* sounded behind. "We're doing two hundred eighty thousand miles per second," Tom figured, "and somebody wants us to move over!" He looked back. "Father!" he gasped. "Hermes! Look at that! Father's laid an egg! How could Sandy have been so wrong? Father's 'Mother.' "

"Not bad for a goose now more than a hundred years old," said Hermes.

Tom gasped. "Hermes! Father hasn't aged a bit. *Neither would Sandy!*" He took a long breath. "Hermes — right vernier thrust. One hundred and eighty degrees."

Stardust One went into a long sweeping turn. "What on Earth are you going to do with her?" Hermes asked, as they headed back to Camelot.

"You mean what am I going to do with her on Earth?" asked Tom. "What you're supposed to do in a situation like this — live happily ever after!"